"Don't ever let me go!"
Sara implored Alex

"Never," Alex whispered harshly, and for a second the silence seemed tense with feeling—a silence shattered by the sound of a car engine.

Alex lifted his head, listening, his body rigid as the car stopped outside the cottage.

He broke away from her and sprang to the window. The next second he was racing out of the room.

Sara was startled. She stumbled out of bed and to the window. There was a small, rakish white sports car, with a woman sliding out of the driver's seat. Sara recognized her immediately. She took a deep breath as the dam broke.

Through the painful rush of memories she heard Alex asking angrily, "What the hell are *you* doing here?"

Books by Charlotte Lamb

A VIOLATION
SECRETS

HARLEQUIN PRESENTS

HARLEQUIN ROMANCE

These books may be available at your local bookseller.

Don't miss any of our special offers. Write to us at the following address for information on our newest releases.

Harlequin Reader Service
P.O. Box 52040, Phoenix, AZ 85072-2040
Canadian address: P.O. Box 2800, Postal Station A,
5170 Yonge St., Willowdale, Ont. M2N 6J3

CHARLOTTE LAMB

sleeping desire

Harlequin Books

TORONTO • NEW YORK • LONDON
AMSTERDAM • PARIS • SYDNEY • HAMBURG
STOCKHOLM • ATHENS • TOKYO • MILAN

Harlequin Presents first edition January 1986
ISBN 0-373-10851-6

Original hardcover edition published in 1985
by Mills & Boon Limited

CHAPTER ONE

'I'LL get rid of my husband if I have to put a bullet through his head!' Sara was too angry to keep her voice down, and too engrossed to realise that she could be heard all over the restaurant, but the man sitting opposite her turned red as heads lifted and people stared, saucer-eyed.

'Sara!' he murmured, giving her a meaning look.

'What?'

'People can hear you,' Peter pointed out, then added quickly as she scowled: 'Don't worry about Stevenson—the divorce will go through, whatever he does to delay it. There's nothing he can do to stop it.'

'He can annoy me! He can refuse to answer letters from my solicitor, fight me every inch of the way over the settlement enquiries. He has a hundred little tricks up his sleeve—you don't know him. Alex gets a kick out of driving people crazy. It's a wonder nobody has murdered him before. I'd be doing mankind—not to mention womankind—a service by shooting him.'

'Forget about him, eat your dinner,' Peter said uneasily, aware of all those curious ears, but she eyed the mouthwatering sole in front of her as if it was rat poison and pushed the plate away, shaking her head.

'Something wrong with the sole?' Peter asked anxiously, peering at it.

'I'm too angry to eat,' Sara said, then softened as she met his mild blue eyes. 'Don't look so worried, Peter, I'm not going to let Alex drive me to desperate measures. He'd love that.'

'We only have to be patient,' Peter reminded her, his gaze on the smooth-skinned cameo of her face as she managed a smile. He was so different from Alex, she thought, with love and an odd sort of relief—Peter was a man with gentle strength, a quiet man with inner reserves of confidence and self-control which she admired and envied. He was attractive without being striking; his features calmly modelled, a wide brow and straight nose, broad cheekbones and a firm mouth. His face could have been placid and even stolid had it not been for the gloss of his thick, sleek blond hair and wide-set blue eyes, which gave him a touch of glamour.

'I'll try,' Sara promised, her mouth wry. 'I'm not famous for my patience, though, and Alex knows just how to get under my skin.'

'I don't see what he thinks he's gaining by these delaying tactics,' Peter murmured as he finished the steak he was eating and leaned back in his chair. 'After all, you've been separated for over a year now. He knows your marriage is over. He hasn't seen you for months or even tried to, has he?' The faint question in his eyes underlined the uncertain note in his voice and Sara smiled at him, shaking her head.

'He knows I can't stand the sight of him—if he

came within a mile of me I'd chuck things at him. That isn't the point—I told you, he loves to needle people. He's bloody-minded. He knows we badly want this divorce so that we can get married, so he is deliberately dragging his feet over every tiny detail. That's the man I married, more fool me. My only excuse is that I was too young to know what I was doing. At nineteen I didn't know my left hand from my right. If my parents had had any sense they would have refused to let me do it, but I suppose I'd have gone ahead whatever they said. I was . . .' She bit off the rest of that sentence, her teeth clenched on words she swallowed just in time. At nineteen she had been fathoms deep in love and she wouldn't have listened to a word anyone said against Alex—that must have been obvious to her parents, not that they had had any doubts either, at the time; they had taken to Alex on sight, he had made sure of that. He could be irresistible when he chose; he should have been an actor not a film director, Sara thought bitterly, he was far too aware of the impression he was giving and much too clever. People tended to believe what Alex wanted them to believe and even those who had known him for years and frequently been driven to the edge of madness by his infuriating tactics, became putty in his hands if he decided to charm them.

The waiter materialised to take their plates, glancing at the half-eaten fish on Sara's with a concerned frown. 'Madame did not like the sole? Could we offer something else?'

She gave the man a polite smile. 'The sole was

delicious but I'm not very hungry. 'I'll just have some coffee now, thank you.'

'So will I,' Peter decided.

With a shrug of resignation the waiter left and Sara laughed softly. 'We've offended him.'

Peter watched her indulgently. 'I'll miss you while I'm in Holland—why don't you come with me? I can easily book another flight and a hotel room for you and when I've finished my business we could spend a couple of days exploring Amsterdam. It's a lovely city, you'd enjoy yourself, there's so much to do there. There's something very special about cities whose streets are canals—Venice and Amsterdam are my favourite places.'

Regretfully, Sara shook her head. 'I'd have loved to, but I promised my mother I'd have lunch there tomorrow. It's their wedding anniversary, didn't I tell you?' Her mother had rung weeks ago to make sure Sara didn't forget the date and it would be impossible to back out now, the whole family would be offended. They took their private rituals seriously in the Calthrop family; everyone would be there tomorrow, her uncle and both aunts, her two brothers and her older sister, Janie.

'Oh, of course! I'd forgotten, stupid of me. I'm sorry,' Peter said at once with understanding. He came from a closely knit family, too; unlike Alex, who had been quite alone in the world, without kith or kin, and apparently in no need of either, which might explain his air of self-sufficiency and that egocentric indifference to everything but his own needs.

'You must show me Amsterdam some other time,' Sara told Peter and he nodded cheerfully.

'I'll do that,' he promised, watching her with an intent gaze. 'You look beautiful tonight,' he said suddenly, and her vivid green eyes melted with warmth and amusement.

'Don't sound so surprised, it's hardly very flattering!' she teased but Peter was in a serious mood.

'I'm always surprised by how lovely you are,' he protested. 'Every time I look at you I find it hard to believe that anyone could be so beautiful.'

'What a nice thing to say,' she said, taken aback, putting out a hand. Peter took it and held it between both his own, his skin warm on hers, as he stared into her oval face, the purity of her features framed in a rich cloud of auburn hair, which tumbled, burnished and gleaming, to her shoulders. Sara somehow contrived to look ethereal when her face was not in motion—when she wasn't talking with vivacity or laughing, but in quiet, pensive mood. She was volatile in temperament, but it was the shape of her face that was largely responsible for sometimes giving the impression that she was not quite of this world. Her cheekbones were so high and slanting, her nose so finely moulded, her temples delicately structured with dark brows perfectly arched above her eyes. When the eye was led down to her mouth, however, a contradiction was evident—Sara's lips were full and sensual, their curves excitingly warm.

'You're a puzzling mixture,' Peter murmured, smiling wryly, as though he wondered, at times, what sort of creature he had caught and meant to marry. They were very different in character; there was something slightly bland and cautious about Peter which was in complete contrast to Sara's explosive mix of high spirits, passion and sensitivity. A few years ago she would have found him boring and become impatient with him, but that was before her battering at Alex Stevenson's hands. She had reeled away, bruised and off balance, and found Peter's quiet nature something of a haven; he made her feel secure, he cosseted and soothed her, gave her the reassurance she hungered for.

'I'm glad I found you,' Peter said, raising her hand to his lips and kissing the soft pink palm.

'So am I,' she agreed whole-heartedly, smiling into his eyes.

The waiter brought their coffee and Peter relinquished her hand; he wasn't a man who liked being stared at or watched and Sara had rapidly learnt not to wear anything too striking. It made Peter self-conscious if men stared at her too avidly, he liked her to wear cool, clear colours and elegant styles which did not draw attention to the explosive curve of her figure. It wasn't so much that he was possessive as that he preferred a very private lifestyle, and in that, too, he was completely the opposite of Alex Stevenson who was as much at home flashing through the jetset world of nightclubs and smart parties as he was in old jeans and chunky sweaters energetically scrubbing the deck of his small boat. Alex had encouraged her to wear colours that hurt the eyes and daring dresses that made men's heads spin.

He had expected her to put on jeans and plimsolls and oilskins to come sailing with him in all sorts of weathers, too. Sara had submissively dressed for him for years until the day when she suddenly looked at herself in a mirror and saw what a puppet she had become, how slavishly she let Alex dictate what she wore and did, how meekly she accepted the way they both lived.

Watching Peter through her lowered lashes now, she reminded herself not to allow that to happen again. It was one thing to dress to please Peter and another never to dress to please herself. She enjoyed it when he stared at her with open admiration but she must not let Peter's opinions rule her whole life.

'What are you thinking?' Peter asked as he finished his coffee and signalled for the bill.

'How much I'll miss you while you're in Amsterdam,' she said with conscious evasion. 'What time does your plane leave?'

'Ten o'clock tomorrow,' he said, paying the bill. 'I'll try to ring you tomorrow night but I may be out late, I'm having dinner with some businessmen who may keep me talking until midnight.'

'I may stay the night with my parents anyway,' said Sara, following him to the door of the restaurant past tables whose occupants glanced up and stared after her as she sauntered through the crowded room. The cream silk dress was stylish and faintly demure but could do little to douse the vibrancy of her sex appeal; her body moved too sensually under the clinging material.

'Oh, you're going for the whole weekend? I

didn't realise.' Peter held the door open for her and she walked through, smiling at him sideways.

'I thought I might—the weather is quite good and it would be fun to spend a weekend by the sea.'

'I may ring you there on Sunday morning, then, but I should be back by mid-week, with any luck. You'll be in the office on Monday?'

'I'd better be or Jaws will swallow me alive.' Sara laughed as she slid into the front passenger seat of Peter's car. She worked in an advertising agency as a copywriter. Her boss, George Jerome, was universally known as Jaws, partly because he had prominent white teeth which he constantly flashed in a predatory smile and partly because he was prone, in a temper, to rend people limb from limb without mercy. He hated people to be unpunctual, that really made him angry.

Peter started the car and drove smoothly away, the street lights gleaming on his sleek blond hair and giving his face an angelic look. 'While you're in that part of the world, check up with the local estate agent and see if your husband has put the cottage on the market yet. As he doesn't answer your solicitor's letters he may not have offered it for sale even now, and you won't get your settlement for months after the divorce is final unless that place has been sold.'

'Yes,' Sara said thoughtfully. 'I'll do that. I don't trust Alex, he's quite capable of ignoring everything we've asked him to do—I wish the cottage had been owned jointly, I could have put it on the market myself, but he owned it before I met him. It's not as if he was living there—he's either in the States or in his London flat. My mother says he rarely goes down to the cottage now.'

'Divorce is a nasty business,' Peter said soberly. 'But you were his wife for five years, you're entitled to a generous settlement.'

She frowned. 'Oh, don't talk about it—I hate the whole sorry mess. I wish we could just forget about the financial side of it.'

'Nonsense,' Peter said. 'Your family gave you a lot of the furniture in the cottage, didn't they? And it was you who looked after the place and did all the redecorating—that was your home as much as his and the law demands a fair division.' He thought for a second, then said: 'I suppose he doesn't intend to give it to you after the divorce? That would explain why he ignores all your solicitor's letters about the financial arrangements.'

'He ignores them to annoy me!' she muttered, her eyes fierce with anger. 'He wouldn't give me anything.'

They pulled up outside the house in which she had a small flat and Peter turned to kiss her lingeringly. When he pulled back his head he smiled down at her, his blue eyes calming. 'I wish I could come in for a while, but I have to pack yet and I must get a good night's sleep or I'll get a headache tomorrow when I fly. Try not to let Stevenson get to you! Ignore him.'

'I'll try,' she said wearily but she had been trying to ignore Alex for the past year and it was very hard to ignore a man who had apparently forgotten she existed. There was no incentive to help her put him out of her mind. At times Sara felt like going along to Alex's flat and chucking a brick through the window, yelling: 'Pretend you haven't noticed that!' He probably would, come to that, he would get a glazier along to replace the glass and put his feet on the table, whistling, while she danced outside like a crazy woman. Alex had a vicious habit of letting his opponent defeat himself—or herself. The angrier she became the more coolly he turned a blind eye to her activities, but she had no intention of committing the final folly of being driven into meeting him face to face to discuss their divorce. That was undoubtedly what Alex was trying to provoke her into doing—but she wasn't getting caught in that trap.

The next day she packed a case and took a taxi to Charing Cross to get a train to the Kent coast. Sara didn't have a car of her own; living in London made it pointless since traffic was impossible and parking even worse. She lived in Camden and took a bus to work. When she had a date with Peter he always drove her home and in an emergency or if she was in a hurry she could always take a taxi. Even if she had had a car it would have been faster and probably cheaper to visit her family by taking the train. Her parents lived in a small village on the edge of Romney Marsh and if Sara was coming down her father always met the train and drove her from the railway station to the family home.

When she came out of the station into bright sunlight she saw her father hurrying out of the car park opposite. Sara waved and John

Calthrop stopped in his tracks briefly, then came forward to take the case out of her hands, saying wryly, 'I'm sorry, I meant to get here ten minutes ago but just as I was leaving we had a 'phone call.'

'Never mind, I've only just arrived anyway.' Sara reached up to kiss him; she had quite a way to reach even standing on tiptoe. John Calthrop was over six foot, a very thin, long-limbed man with hair like spilt marmalade, orange, and streaky now with threads of silver. He had hazel eyes and bushy eyebrows which had turned completely silver several years ago but in spite of that his face was very young. He had an agile mind, adaptable and lively, and no intention of getting old before he had no choice. In his fifties, he had taken up jogging and squash and had learnt to play the guitar last year. He claimed that he kept himself young by learning at least one new thing a year.

'You look sensational,' he told his younger daughter as Sara got into the front seat of his immaculately kept but aged white Volkswagen, affectionately known to the family as Lady because John Calthrop felt it had to be a lucky car to have survived so long. 'She's a lucky little lady,' he had kept saying as year after year saw the old car still going strong, and Lady she had remained to them all. Watching her father pat the car's gleaming bonnet Sara hoped it would keep going for ever. John Calthrop loved that car.

As they drove out of the car park and headed for White Abbas, the village in which the Calthrops lived, Sara asked her father how the rest of the family were and he talked cheerfully while he drove.

'The shop still doing well?' she asked.

'We don't make a fortune but it's enough for us,' her father said. He owned a chemist's shop in Rye, the nearest town of any size, and drove there and back each day across the Romney Marsh, along winding, hedge-lined little roads with flat damp fields on either side, the rich grass cropped by placid white sheep. The marsh was scattered with medieval churches, their white spires the most useful landmark by which a stranger could steer his way through that bewildering, low-lying district, which had once lain under the sea and been drained centuries ago to make some of the best grazing land in the country.

Sara felt a qualm of nostalgia as she looked around while they drove; she had lived on the marsh for most of her life, she knew these wandering lanes by heart, she had cycled around them as a child, driven around them with Alex after they were married. She had been married in the church just in the centre of the tiny village. She looked briefly at the green turf lapping the walls, the grey tombstones and shadowy yew trees, the dark layered cedar leaning against the ancient dry stone wall enclosing the churchyard. A few sheep were ambling between the graves, heads down to nibble the grass. Sara sighed and her father gave her a quick, concerned look.

'Tired?' He skated enquiry over her oval face and Sara immediately smiled to disguise her real feelings.

'London does that to you—it's good to be home for a few days.'

'You look more like your mother every day,' John Calthrop said, turning up a steep lane which led out of the village, and Sara laughed, shaking her head.

'Couldn't we drive along the old sea road?' Sara asked casually and felt her father looking at her averted profile.

'I promised your mother I'd get you home in time for lunch—the new road is so much quicker.' The villagers still called the lane 'the new road' although it had been used for several hundred years. It took a short cut over a hill above the sea, whereas the old sea road curved along beside the beach and, in spring, was often lashed by wild tides which crashed over the stone sea wall, flinging stones and wet seaweed across the tarmac, leaving the road under several feet of water. Unwary cars had been overturned or had windows broken, one or two people had been killed by being trapped by an unexpectedly high tide, but locals knew better than to use the road when a high spring tide was expected, and automatically took the new road in preference unless they wanted to go down to the sea.

'I wanted to see the cottage,' Sara admitted flatly. 'Is there a For Sale board up outside it yet?'

'I haven't been down that way for a while,' John Calthrop said.

Sara shot him a questioning look. She knew perfectly well that if the cottage was on the market her father would soon have heard;

nothing much happened on the Marsh without everyone for miles knowing all about it. The villages were close-knit, small communities and the Calthrops had lived there for years—they knew everyone and everyone knew them.

Her father was being evasive—why? Had Alex been here recently, had he confided in her parents? She had deliberately tried not to involve her family in the quarrel between herself and Alex because she knew how much they all liked him, but was Alex so diplomatic? Her father was a particular friend of his; they had often sailed together in Alex's boat, or taken walks across the marsh to fish or watch herons nesting among the tall reeds beside some slow-moving stream. John Calthrop knew all the long-legged birds' favourite nesting sites, he had taught Alex how to creep stealthily through the sedge without disturbing the herons, they had spent hours crouching down to watch the birds rise, flapping, long legs trailing, in search of food for their young. Sara uneasily watched her father and saw from his profile that he was just as uneasy. She couldn't talk to him about Alex, she recognised again, she couldn't drag her family into that private little war, it wasn't fair to them. Alex might have no such scruples, but Sara refused to descend to his level.

John Calthrop turned in at an open gate, the car bumped along a rough driveway and pulled up outside an old stone house with a weathered, mossy roof. Sara jumped out just as her mother appeared in the doorway, waving.

'I wondered what had happened to you, I

expected you a quarter of an hour ago,' Molly Calthrop said, hugging her daughter.

'We aren't late,' Sara said. 'Your clock must be wrong.'

Her father had pulled the suitcase out of the boot of his car, he passed them, grinning. 'Your mother can't wait for anything,' he commented and Molly Calthrop flapped her apron at him like someone shooing hens.

If Sara had inherited her colouring from her father she had got her physical build from her mother. Molly Calthrop was fair and blue-eyed with delicate features and a very feminine figure. Even at fifty she looked like a young woman from a distance; you had to be very close to see the faint lines on her face. She was a very practical woman, lively, warm-hearted, always busy. She had married very young and been contented all her life—and that showed in her face and smiling eyes.

'Everyone here?' Sara asked as they went into the house.

'You're the last to arrive,' Molly said, chuckling. 'I'll have to put up a House Full sign! Janie's in the kitchen cooking the lunch with me and Ann's upstairs feeding Little John—wait until you see that child, he looks just like Robert at that age. Stephanie's out in the garden with James and the two little girls, playing rounders.' She walked into the kitchen and Sara grinned at her older sister as Janie swung, a gravy dish in one hand and a spoon in the other, to greet her.

'Well, that's a relief, now we can start dishing

up this lunch—Mum wouldn't hear of it until you arrived.'

'Smells delicious!' Sara said. 'Can I help?'

'No, everything's ready.' Janie was more like their father than Sara, she was tall and thin with distinctly ginger hair and hazel eyes. She had been married for ten years and had one daughter, who must be out in the garden, although Janie's husband, Ralph, was currently in India for three months, doing some research. He was an expert on tropical diseases, a doctor who worked not on patients but with a microscope in laboratories, doing endless repetitive experiments to discover the answers to some hitherto unanswered questions about diseases in places like India and the East. Whenever Sara saw him she marvelled that someone as cheerful and schoolboyish as Ralph could do such intricate, painstaking work.

'Call everyone in from the garden, would you, Sara?' Mrs Calthrop asked, draining some vegetables at the sink. 'Make sure the children wash their hands.'

'Does that include James and Steffy?' Sara asked teasingly, opening the kitchen window and yelling: 'Lunch!'

It was a very happy day. The house was crammed with people, but they all got on very well, and the weather was perfect for early June— the air warm, filled with languor, far too good to stay indoors, so they went for a walk across the flat marshy fields taking a picnic with them. They settled in a sloping meadow rich with daisies and buttercups; the children played with a ball or made daisy chains, the men went for a walk to try and spot a kingfisher which often lurked there along the stream. The women talked and kept an eye on the wicker picnic basket in which the children showed far too much interest. Sara lay down on the sweet-smelling grass and closed her eyes, feeling the sun on her face, listening to the lazy voices and laughter. Ever since she left Alex she had felt oddly excluded from the usual family chatter; divorce was something that threatened and worried her family, they found it hard to like Peter as much as they had liked Alex in spite of all Peter's efforts to get on with them. Sara felt uneasy whenever she mentioned Peter, a silence always fell, people looked down or avoided her eyes.

Summer was at its richest; the hedges foamed with white May flowers, cowslips showed gold among the vivid new grass, the ditches were full of gently waving white saxifrage and Jack-by-the-hedge, which the children mistook for nettles, screaming when the hairy leaves touched them.

While they ate the picnic later, a cuckoo called among the hazels in a nearby copse but a moment later the echoing note came from more distant fields where the soft blue haze of a late summer afternoon was thickening towards twilight.

Sara felt sleepy, flushed with country air and exercise; she helped the other women pack the wicker basket with the uneaten food and then they started to walk back, the children running on ahead, calling to each other, the men strolling behind, their deeper voices casual and contented.

Sara had given her parents a set of crystal wine-glasses as an anniversary present. That

evening, before the rest of the family set off for
home, they all drank a toast from the glasses. The
children lay half-asleep in chairs, yawning, the
lavender of dusk had fallen outside the window.
Everyone was cheerful and tired. For some stupid
reason that made Sara want to cry; her eyes felt
hot and weary. She couldn't wait to get to bed,
she wanted to sleep for days.

Sunday morning dawned cool and misty. After
a light breakfast Sara decided to walk down to
the sea along the narrow, winding road which
plunged down the hill and curled round beside
the beach. She wanted to see her old cottage, she
hadn't been near the place for months and she
didn't think Alex came down very often. She was
the only one who had stayed the night. When she
said she was going for a walk her parents looked
at each other, then hurriedly offered to come, too.

'I'm walking down to the sea,' Sara said
casually.

'Why don't we walk over to the village?' Mrs
Calthrop suggested, too quickly.

Sara gave her a dry smile, shaking her head. 'I
want to see if there's a For Sale sign on the
cottage.'

Her mother sighed. 'There isn't,' she admitted,
then she looked at John Calthrop. 'She ought to
be told,' she said.

'What?' Sara asked.

'Now, Molly, stay out of it,' John Calthrop
said.

'What are you talking about?' asked Sara.

'I don't like plots,' Molly Calthrop complained.

'What plot?' Sara felt the back of her neck prickle. 'What is Alex up to?' she demanded.

'It is none of our business,' John Calthrop told his wife, not looking at his daughter.

'Are you and Alex plotting against me?' Sara demanded, her eyes turning bottle green with temper, and her mother looked unhappily at her.

'Of course not, Sara, how can you say that? But poor Alex . . .'

'Poor Alex?' repeated Sara disbelievingly. 'Poor Alex?'

'He's all alone in the world,' her mother reproached her, eyes wide. 'He thinks of us as his family, you know, not having any family of his own.'

'Poor little orphan Alex,' Sara said scathingly. 'Don't make me cry. He's about as pathetic as a well-fed boa constrictor and if he fed you a line about being lonely and misunderstood it was because he knew you were soft-hearted enough to fall for it. He wouldn't try that stuff on me, he knows I'd see through him too fast.' She fixed her eyes on them unblinkingly. 'So what is he plotting? Come on, Mum, tell me!'

Molly Calthrop looked at her husband, her face confused and uncertain, and he shrugged, making a wry face.

'If you think she ought to know, tell her.'

Mrs Calthrop looked at Sara. 'Alex is at the cottage,' she said and Sara took an unsteady breath, her ears buzzing with shock.

'Now? He's there now?' She looked hard at them both and her father looked away. 'You were going to let me go over there without telling me

I'd be bound to walk straight into him?' Her eyes accused and Mrs Calthrop looked even more unhappy.

'Well, you know now, it's your decision whether you see him or not,' her mother murmured.

Sara went on staring at her father. 'Is he planning to come here today? Is that what you had fixed up between you? You would spring him on me without warning?'

'There was no plot,' her father said, shifting impatiently in his chair, a frown on his face. 'I simply think it's time you talked to him, face to face, instead of all this nonsense about solicitors' letters and divorce settlements. The man's your husband, Sara. However angry you are with him, you can't get away from that. What harm would it do to see him, talk like two sane adults?'

'He's conned you as much as he has Mum,' Sara said explosively. 'I am not seeing him. Have you forgotten that he took his secretary to Singapore with him for a fortnight after he had told me he was going alone? Her husband divorced her, *he* was convinced Alex had had an affair with her and she didn't deny it. If it hadn't been true, wouldn't she have said so?'

Mr Calthrop looked at her with uncertainty. 'Alex told me it was all lies.'

'She was there, Dad—he can't deny that. The hotel register had her name in it and she was in the next room to Alex with a communicating door between them, a door which one of the hotel staff saw open when he took up drinks one evening. That was good enough for her husband

and it's good enough for me.' Sara's voice was
hard with bitter anger, her face darkly flushed.
She hated talking about the past but they had
forced her hand; they had let Alex talk them into
accepting his version of the events which had
made Sara leave him. He could be very
persuasive, very convincing, but Sara wasn't
going to let him have a chance to coax her into
forgetting his affair with his secretary.

'I'd better take an early train back to town,' she
decided sharply and her mother moved protest-
ingly.

'Oh, that isn't necessary. If you really won't
see Alex then . . .'

'If he knows I'm here he'll find a way of
getting to me unless I leave now,' Sara said. 'I'll
go and pack. I'm sorry, Mum, but I won't be
coerced into seeing him.'

She went upstairs, trembling with shock and
anger, and hurriedly packed her case. The lazy,
relaxed atmosphere had been wrecked, and she
had been shaken by her father's attitude to Alex.
He was obviously half inclined to take Alex's
side—heaven knew what Alex had been telling
him. Her father might be able to forgive Alex for
having been unfaithful, but Sara burned with
anger whenever she thought of it. She had always
believed—childishly, perhaps—that her parents
would support her against anyone else. How
could they listen to Alex? How could they
conspire with him to bring them together again?
She felt betrayed, abandoned, she didn't know
whether to cry or smash things.

Her mother had obviously been crying when

she got back downstairs with her case. Sara looked at her ruefully and hugged her. 'I'm sorry I was bad-tempered, don't be upset. I'll be down again soon, but, please—no more plotting with Alex.'

'It was only for you,' her mother wailed, incoherently muttering something about things being such a muddle and Sara didn't understand.

'I do understand, you're fond of him, it's easy for you,' Sara said wildly, then kissed her and said in a husky voice: 'Oh, I must go! I'm sorry.' She fled and her father followed her heavily and drove her in a difficult silence back to the station to catch the late morning train.

On the platform they stood side by side in the misty peace of a half-deserted railway station, saying nothing. Only when the train sluggishly drew up beside them did Sara turn and kiss her father and John Calthrop say: 'I'm sorry, Sara, we didn't mean to upset you, we did it for the best.'

'I know,' she said, because however angry she was with Alex she knew that her parents loved her and wanted her to be happy, but sometimes interference can do more harm than good, they didn't know what they were getting into when they supported Alex.

She leant out of the window, waving, until her father was lost to sight, and then sank back into a window seat. She had chosen an empty carriage and had a pile of magazines to read, but at first she merely stared out at the mist-shrouded fields rushing past. The train put on more speed as it left the coast and headed for Ashford, its first stop on the way to London. Sara couldn't see beyond the nearest fields; the downs were almost invisible in the sea mist which had crept inland and the shapes of houses, trees, barns and horses flashed out of the damp white mist briefly before disappearing into it again.

The train was going much too fast for comfort, the rocking motion made Sara close her eyes. She had a sense of painful relief at having escaped the risk of seeing Alex again. It would have been intolerable—how could her parents have imagined she would agree to talk to him? Of course, there was so much that she had never told them, things she hated to talk about and found painful to remember. Perhaps it was time they knew everything; why should Alex succeed in persuading them to conspire with him against her when, if they knew the whole truth, they wouldn't want to see him either?

She shuddered, opening her eyes, and at that second the train came to a grinding, crashing halt that sounded like the end of the world. Sara was flung sideways across the carriage, desperately trying to save herself by clutching at the seat, but the force of the impact sent her helplessly smashing towards the carriage door, head on, her body tumbling across the floor a second later, arms and legs splayed wide as if she were a rag doll some careless child had thrown away.

CHAPTER TWO

WHEN Sara managed to open her eyes again, she became immediately conscious of two things—firstly, her head was throbbing with a sick agonising beat, and secondly a strange man was kneeling beside her watching her anxiously. He was middle-aged and grey-haired and wore a dark uniform that seemed vaguely familiar. Sara screwed up her eyes to see him better; everything was very misty and she couldn't see very clearly.

'What . . . happened?' she whispered.

'You'll be all right, Miss,' the man promised but somehow he didn't sound too certain of that.

'Where . . .' she began and forgot what she had meant to ask, her mind seemed to have trouble concentrating. She put a shaky hand up to her head. The man tried to stop her but was too late—as her fingers dropped Sara saw the blood on them and her eyes widened in shock.

'I'm bleeding,' she told him stupidly.

'A doctor will be here soon,' the man said and Sara closed her eyes because the mist was getting thicker and she was very tired.

She became conscious again when a doctor in a white coat shone a light into her eyes. Sara frowned and stared at him crossly. Why had he woken her up in the middle of the night? 'Why am I in hospital?' she asked and he looked interested. 'Tell me if this hurts,' he murmured, gently wiping her temples with something cool and moist while he studied the source of the bleeding.

'It hurts,' Sara said through her teeth, looking away from his abstracted face and finding herself looking at a cow which was leaning over a hedge with calm curiosity, watching them. 'What is that cow doing in hospital?' Sara asked the doctor who sat back on his heels and considered her with even deeper interest.

'Cow?' he enquired guardedly. 'You can see cows?'

'Behind you,' Sara said and with a start he looked round and then grinned, becoming unexpectedly human.

'You had me worried for a minute!' he said. 'Where's that stretcher?' he called to someone out of sight.

'Ready when you are, doctor,' a voice said cheerfully.

The doctor produced a roll of bandage and began delicately wrapping white gauze around Sara's head, his fingers deft and light.

'What happened?' Sara asked him, realising suddenly that she was lying on the floor of the train—she couldn't remember how she had got there or where she had been going but although the angle was unfamiliar there was no doubt that she was in a railway carriage and a file of people were passing along the track outside the open door. She heard voices, felt people looking into the carriage curiously. 'Was it a train crash?' she asked the doctor.

'You don't remember?'

'Would I ask if I did?' she muttered crossly, then asked: 'What's wrong with me? Am I badly hurt?'

'A few bruises and bumps, and one would expect those,' the doctor said soothingly. 'You've banged your head, there's a nasty cut across the forehead, but we'll have the head X-rayed as soon as we get you to a hospital. No need to get worried, I'm sure it isn't serious, a few stitches and you'll be as right as rain, Miss . . .?'

'Mrs,' Sara said. 'Mrs Stevenson,' and then thought very slowly and said: 'My husband . . .' She seemed to be in a stupid state, she couldn't finish the sentence.

'Yes? He wasn't with you? You want us to ring him and tell him what has happened?' the doctor guessed reassuringly. 'Of course, don't worry, someone will let him know.'

Sara's brow furrowed. Was that what she had wanted to say? She was too dizzy to say anything else as they lifted her on to a stretcher and carried her along the misty track to a waiting ambulance. After they had slid Sara into it a nurse climbed in with her and the doors shut.

As they drove away Sara asked: 'Were many people hurt?'

'A few people have shock and bruises, but nothing serious,' the nurse said cheerfully, taking her pulse. 'You were our only real casualty, thank heavens, and you've only bumped your head a bit.'

'Lucky me,' Sara said drily, closing her eyes. 'Where are you taking me? Which hospital?'

'Willesborough, do you know it?'

Sara did and nodded, flinching as the movement made a sharp pain jab along the front of her temples. While they drove to the hospital she tried hard to remember where she had been going in the train, but it hurt to think. She was confused and vague, something was bothering her, that was all she knew. Something to do with Alex—but what?

While she was being admitted to a quiet casualty ward she kept trying to remember what had happened before she got on the train. Had Alex driven her to the station? Was he at home in the cottage? She couldn't even remember the day or what had happened recently, there was a terrifying blackness in the forefront of her mind.

She was reluctant to mention it to the nurse who admitted her, producing a form and asking her a series of questions. The lapse of memory was bound to pass in a few hours, Sara told herself; it must be a temporary side effect of the shock of the train crash. The few odd blank spots were quite meaningless and unimportant—she remembered everything that mattered about herself, Alex, her family. She simply couldn't remember silly little things, like what day it was or what had happened yesterday. Some instinct stopped her talking about it; it worried and frightened her. The doctors at the hospital might think she had gone crazy, but she felt quite clear and lucid except where the last few days were concerned. She knew it was summer, she knew she must have been going up to London to shop or perhaps meet Alex. It would come back to her, she assured herself, so instead of panicking she took hold of herself and answered the nurse's questions calmly, trying to sound quite normal.

'Name?'

'Sara Stevenson.'

'Married?'

'Yes.'

'Next of kin is your husband? What's his name?'

'Alex Stevenson.'

'Address?' Sara gave it and the nurse asked: 'Telephone number?' Sara gave that and the nurse asked: 'Age? Date of birth?' and when Sara had rattled them off looked at her with a smile, writing down the date of birth in an inexplicably quizzical way. 'Can't count?' she said cheerfully but before Sara could ask her what she meant by that, the nurse asked for the name of her own doctor, and told her that she would be going down to X-ray immediately.

The nurse then produced a wheelchair and Sara reluctantly sat down in it. She was even more reluctant when the nurse insisted on folding a red blanket over her. 'It's a warm day,' she protested.

'You may have shock,' the nurse explained. 'You're not showing any signs of it yet but it could be delayed shock, we don't want you catching cold.'

Sara saw there was no point in arguing. She was wheeled down long corridors and deposited in the X-ray department. After she had had her head X-rayed from various angles she was taken to a waiting-room and given a cup of tea while the doctor on duty examined the X-ray films. It must have been half an hour later when Sara saw him. Cheerfully he told her that there was no sign of any internal damage; the surface cut on the temples was the only injury.

'You've been very lucky,' he said. 'There's no need for you to stay in here. You can go home when you've had some stitches in that cut, but of course if you have any headaches or feel dizzy or have any problems with your eyesight, come back at once.'

Sara frowned. 'Will I have a scar?'

He gave her a faint smile. 'A very small one but you can always wear your hair over it; cultivate a fringe.'

Sara flinched as she saw the instrument a nurse was wheeling towards them. 'Will it hurt?'

'You're not a baby, are you?' the doctor teased. 'Don't worry, I'll give you a local anaesthetic, you won't feel a thing.'

He warned her to keep very still while he was stitching the cut, and Sara closed her eyes and tried to pretend nothing was happening. She heard the doctor ask the nurse: 'Have her relatives been told?'

'Her husband is coming to collect her,' the nurse said and Sara breathed a sigh of relief.

When Alex got here she could let him take charge, she needn't feel so confused and uncertain any more. She felt intensely isolated in this strange environment among all these strange people; she wanted Alex here to give her reassurance, to deal with these intangible problems. She could tell Alex that she couldn't

remember the past few days, that she didn't know
why she had been on that train or where she had
been going. Alex would know what to do, he
would look after her, he always did.

When the doctor had finished stitching the
wound, he washed his hands at a sink in the
corner of the room, talking to her while the nurse
bandaged her head again.

'Now when you get home I want you to rest as
much as possible—no sudden movement, no
exercise for the moment. Stay in bed for a couple
of days and come back to have those stitches out
next week. Ask the receptionist to make an
appointment for you.'

The nurse took her off to have another cup of
tea and left her in the waiting-room with some
magazines. Sara couldn't concentrate on them,
she flicked over the glossy pages absently for a
while and then leaned back in her chair, her eyes
closed, her temples numb and cold under the
bandage.

When she heard the door open her eyes opened
too, looking quickly towards the door. 'Alex!' she
said on a shaky note, getting up too quickly. Her
head spun and she swayed and Alex crossed the
room in two long-legged strides to catch hold of
her.

She leaned on his wide shoulder, trying to
smile. 'It's the shock,' she whispered to excuse
the trembling of her body.

'Are you okay?' he asked and his voice was
odd, husky, almost hesitant. Sara sensed that he
was worried about her and wound her arm round
his slim waist, letting her weight fall on him,

intensely glad to have that strength of his to lean
on.

'I am now you're here,' she said, smiling, and
felt his lean body tense against her. 'Don't worry,
Alex!' she added quickly. 'Just take me home—I
want to get out of here, I hate hospitals, always
have. They're very kind, but there's something
about the smell of disinfectant and floor polish
that makes me go weak at the knees.'

'I thought it was just me that made you go
weak at the knees,' he said softly, his cheek
brushing the untidy cloud of her auburn hair.

She gave a rather wavering smile up at him and
experienced the sharp jab of pleasure she always
felt when she saw him, she had never quite got
used to the instant impact of his looks. It wasn't
simply his height or the powerful elegance of his
long body; she sometimes thought that if you
only saw Alex's eyes you would tremble at the
force of his personality. She looked into them
now, riveted; he had the eyes of some predatory
creature, a fierce hawk, the iris gold-brown and
gleaming, the pupil as black as his jet black hair.

'Take me home,' she whispered as his head
bent towards her and he straightened again and
steered her silently to the door.

The nurse on duty at the reception desk called
them over to sign for Sara's possessions, which
had been brought with her in the ambulance.
Alex signed the form while Sara stared, frowning,
at the small suitcase. Why had she had that with
her? Had she been going to stay overnight in
London? She had had the case for several years
and usually took it when she was only going to be

away for a night or two. But where on earth could she have been going?

Alex had parked his car a few feet from the hospital entrance. He helped her into the passenger seat and got in beside her after locking her suitcase in the boot of his car. As they drove out of the gates Sara gave a deep sigh, feeling lighter, as though a weight had dropped from her shoulders.

'Do my parents know?' she asked, closing her eyes and letting her head fall back against the seat.

'Yes, I told them,' Alex said coolly. 'They were worried at first, but the hospital had told me you weren't seriously injured and your parents agreed that I should come alone. It didn't seem a good idea for you to have the whole pack of us turning up.'

She smiled, well able to imagine how agitated her mother would have been. 'I had four stitches in my head,' she told Alex a moment later. 'It didn't hurt, they'd given me an anaesthetic, but it left me feeling very odd—a bit light-headed. I can't feel my forehead at all, it's quite numb.'

'I don't think you should talk,' Alex said carefully. 'The doctor told me you ought to have plenty of rest and quiet. When we get home you're to go to bed and stay there for a couple of days.'

'Yes, he told me that.' Sara wanted to talk, though; she was disturbed by this odd blankness in her memory, she had to tell someone about it because it was preying on her mind and she was getting very up-tight about it. Alex would know what to do, whether she should tell the doctor. Sara didn't want to have to go back to the hospital, she felt tired and a little weak, but she imagined that was purely the shock of the accident. Once that had worn off surely her memory would return in full? The things she had forgotten were so unimportant; what could have happened in the last few days that had any significance? Her daily life was always peaceful; a matter of happy routine. If Alex was at home she cooked his meals and went sailing or walking with him, spent all her time with him. If he was working abroad she did the housework and gardening, visited her family, read, watched television and talked to Alex on the 'phone each evening, wrote him a letter before she went to sleep.

She suddenly had a brief flash of memory, seeing herself with a paintbrush standing on a trestle in the small study, carefully painting the woodwork, her auburn hair covered by a striped cotton scarf tied gypsy-fashion at the nape. When had she done that? Last week? She frowned, trying to remember more—had she finished decorating the study?

Staring absently out of the car window she saw a bay colt in a field toss its head and gallop away, pretending to be frightened of Alex's silver car as it shot past the field gate. She remembered hanging the new wallpaper in the study; it was green and gold, she had picked it out while Alex was away somewhere. In Rome? she thought, tracking the memory down with difficulty. The car slowed to go through a village; gardens in flower with white lilac and rhododendrons, plastered walls and red brick cottages, a village green on which a sedate game of cricket was in progress, white-flannelled figures moving across the grass while a scattering of people watched, clapping. It was all so familiar, yet she wasn't reassured—she felt a strange pressure inside her head, she was conscious of an intermittent flare of panic without knowing what exactly scared her. It was unnerving not to remember what happened yesterday, the day before, it made her feel incomplete, insecure.

'Alex, I'm worried,' she began nervously, turning to look at his profile, and saw it stiffen in tension, his jawline taut, his mouth rigid, almost as though he knew. Sara stammered. 'I . . . it . . . it may sound silly, but something odd seems to . . . you see, I can't . . .' She swallowed, it was suddenly too hard to say. 'Can't remember,' she whispered and her hand groped for Alex's strong fingers on the driving wheel.

They lifted, took hold of her hand, held it firmly, his skin warm and his grip comforting enough for her to add in a shaky pretence of amusement: 'Stupid, isn't it? I simply can't remember what happened.'

'Well, that's not unusual,' Alex soothed, his thumb slowly stroking the back of her hand. 'One often has a temporary amnesia after a shock—it's only the mind protecting itself, happens all the time. It will pass, everything will come back to you.'

Another car came round a corner just in front of them, screeching on three wheels at around eighty miles an hour, and Alex hurriedly dropped her hand and seized the steering wheel with both hands to steer them out of danger. The car flashed past and Alex snarled an angry comment after it.

'Damned fool! He could have killed us.'

Sara was trembling, she slid down into the seat, her skin cold, the near miss leaving her in a state of near panic. Alex looked sideways at her quickly and frowned.

'Are you all right?' His deep, husky voice was anxious.

She tried to laugh. 'I'm fine, it gave me a shock—that car . . . silly, isn't it? My nerves have been shot to pieces, and not being able to remember some things makes me so worried.'

'At least you remembered me,' Alex said lightly but with an odd undertone in his voice and she looked at him with a crooked little smile.

'Whatever else I forgot, I'd never forget you, darling!' She often found it hard to believe that there had ever been a time in her life when she had not known Alex. She had had a very happy childhood, had passed through a contented, uneventful adolescence; dated a few boys between studying for exams and beginning a career as a reporter on a small local newspaper, but the boyfriends she had had before meeting Alex hadn't made much impact on her, she barely remembered their names now and probably wouldn't recognise them if she met them in the street. Emotionally, her whole life had begun the day she met Alex. Until that moment she had been a young, inexperienced, unawakened girl who had not yet discovered her own sexual potential. Alex had made her a woman, a totally fulfilled and contented woman. In a very real sense, Alex *was* her life—nothing in the world mattered as much to her as he did. If she forgot everything, even her own name, she knew she would never forget him.

She let her head fall on his shoulder, rubbing her cheek against the smooth white material of his jacket. 'I love you,' she said, closing her eyes and smiling.

Alex was silent but she felt his lips briefly skate over her mouth, then he concentrated on his driving. They were almost home, she could smell the salty wind blowing from the sea. It was a languid summer afternoon, the air rippled her loose auburn hair, sent it floating backwards as the car put on more speed.

Sara was so worn out that she almost fell asleep, when the car slowed and stopped she started awake with a nervous jolt and sat up. They parked outside the cottage; she smelt the heavy sweetness of lilac and honeysuckle and heard the gulls screaming overhead.

Alex got out and walked round to her side of the car. 'I think I'd better carry you,' he said, his mouth warmly mocking as he slid an arm around her.

She laughed, her hand clasping his brown neck. Alex had carried her into the cottage the day they arrived back from their honeymoon in the Bahamas; it had been autumn then and the trees had been bare, a stiff wind blowing from the sea and a high tide rolling up the beach only minutes away from their front door. She had been shy and uncertain, afraid that after the two enchanting weeks of their honeymoon Alex might soon grow bored with the everyday reality of married life. She felt almost as shy now, which was ridiculous. They had been married for four years, why was she blushing like a schoolgirl and hiding her face on his shoulder?

'This is the second time you've carried me over this threshold,' she reminded him huskily as he found the key, put it into the lock and opened the front door.

Alex looked down at her through thick black lashes, an intimate glance that held invitation. Her heart missed a beat and she was startled by the peculiar speeding up of her pulse rate. It must be an odd side-effect of her recent accident that was creating such turmoil in her senses, she hadn't felt quite so sensually aware of Alex for a long time. Familiarity seemed to blunt the stabs of desire which she had felt during the first year of their marriage, she couldn't remember the last time she had felt her head swim when Alex smiled at her.

'Last time I carried you in here, I got a kiss,' he pointed out smokily, his head descending. Sara lifted her mouth and felt his lips seducing hers to part, the warm invasion arousing and yet oddly tentative, as though Alex was afraid to let passion flare between them.

He breathed thickly as he carried her up the stairs. Sara watched his face from an odd angle, seeing his strong jaw and mouth, the tension of cheekbones and hooded eyes. Alex's face was such a familiar territory to her, yet for some strange reason he looked alien and bewildering at that moment. The carved lids over his golden-brown eyes seemed to be hiding something from her, she saw a tiny tic beating in his cheek and the blue vein in his throat was pulsing more rapidly than usual. Alex was more worried than he was letting her see. It must have been a shock to him when the hospital rang to tell him she had had an accident; he must have wondered how serious it really was, and Sara snuggled closer to him, weak with love because Alex had been frightened for her.

He laid her on the large double bed and Sara lay looking up at him, smiling. 'Was my weight too much for you?' she teased because he was breathing oddly. 'Find me a nightie, will you, darling?' she added as he straightened.

His lashes flickered down against his tanned cheek. She saw a faint redness creep along his cheekbones and looked at him in surprise as he visibly hesitated, but without a word he went across the room to the fitted wardrobe lining one wall and began opening drawers and rummaging among the contents.

Sara laughed, amused. 'Don't tell me you've forgotten where I keep them? Why is it that men never remember where anything is? They're all in the top drawer, where they always are.' She sat up, very carefully, afraid of any sudden movement after the doctor's warnings, and began to unbutton her lemon silk blouse. She grimaced as she saw some drops of blood on the fine silk. There were dusty stains on the sleeves too, no doubt from the floor of the railway carriage. She removed the blouse and unzipped her elegant grey jersey skirt just as Alex turned with a white silk nightdress in his hand.

'This one okay?' He sounded relieved to have finally found the lingerie drawer.

Sara looked at the nightdress in surprise. 'Where did that come from? That isn't mine.'

'Of course it is—I gave it to you one Christmas,' Alex said. 'There was a set—nightdress and négligé in a box. Do you want the négligé too?'

He walked towards her as he spoke and she looked at him questioningly, wondering what other unimportant memories she had lost, then she felt the brooding darkness of Alex's eyes on her slender body in the delicate lace-trimmed slip and everything else drained out of her mind. She was astonished to feel herself trembling as if desire was completely foreign to her, as if no man had ever touched her before, and Alex dropped the nightdress on the bed casually then knelt beside her and gently took her mouth, his cool fingers sliding down her bare arm and closing around the warm flesh of her breast in an intimate touch which made her groan huskily under the probe of his lips.

She drew back laughing unsteadily. 'Darling, I'd love to—but the doctor warned me against exercise of any sort.' Her green eyes teased and Alex grimaced, breathing with uneven rapidity again.

'Yes, you're right—he warned me, too. Get into the nightie and into bed and I'll bring you up some scrambled egg and warm milk, then you had better get some sleep.'

'If I can,' Sara mocked, picking up the delicate nightdress. Alex walked to the door, glancing back once with dark-eyed absorption at her slim body as she stripped off the rest of her underwear and put on the nightie. 'No peeping Toms allowed,' Sara said, sliding down under the covers, blowing him a kiss as he went out. She smiled as she heard him taking the stairs two at a time, but the smile died on her lips a second later. She had forgotten the nightdress Alex had given her—what else had slipped through the torn mesh of her memory? How long would it be before she got her memories back? Alex was making light of it but she sensed his wariness, his uncertainty and the underlying anxiety which was making him so tense all the time. Poor Alex, he hid it well and she was grateful to him for pretending it was perfectly normal and nothing to be alarmed about—but he couldn't hide his real feelings from her. She knew him too well. Alex was far too tense, he had been from the moment he walked into the waiting-room at the hospital. Had the doctor told her the whole truth? Had the X-rays shown some injury that they hadn't told her about? What was Alex keeping from her?

CHAPTER THREE

SARA woke up with a start as a warm body slid into the bed beside her. For a second she was disorientated then she murmured sleepily: 'Alex?'

He lay still, on his side, facing her, moonlight glimmering over the walls and showing her the dark bulk of his head. 'Yes, go back to sleep,' he whispered, but his hand touched the curve of her silk-clad hip and she sensed the unsteadiness of his fingers, smiling to herself. When he brought her the supper he had cooked, Alex hadn't taken his eyes off her, watching her eat the light, scrambled eggs and sip the warm milk, as though every movement she made fascinated him. It was very rare for Alex to go into a kitchen, he saw that as her province. If he was indulging her to the extent of cooking a meal and feeding her forkfuls of scrambled egg, as if she was a child, he must really be worried about her. Sara found that moving; she never doubted that Alex loved her but he hated to show his feelings too openly.

She turned on to her other side and fitted her body into the supportive curve of Alex's body, feeling the warmth of his skin against her back. He slid his arm round her, his hand splayed across her midriff just below her breasts. His face nuzzled among her hair, then he kissed her bare nape. 'Good night,' he murmured and Sara closed her eyes. 'Good night.'

She couldn't get back to sleep, though; her mind, once woken, had begun working on the problem of her lost memories. Why couldn't she remember the last few days? Alex had said he had given her the nightdress at Christmas, she thought back to that time, it seemed as good a starting point as any. They had spent Christmas here at the cottage, just the two of them, and walked up to have Boxing Day lunch with her parents. The weather had been bright and cold, she remembered that walk, their laughter when they saw two yellow-beaked gulls squabbling over a fish head, flapping and fighting, until they both flew away. What had she given Alex? Several books for his enormous collection on the cinema, a new recording of modern jazz? Yes, that had been it—and Alex had given her a whole shower of gifts, she had been unwrapping them for ages while he watched and enjoyed her surprise and enjoyment. Alex was generous, he liked to give her things. There had been so many presents that perhaps it wasn't surprising that she didn't remember the nightdress.

She felt so safe and warm inside his arm, hearing him breathing just behind her, his long thigh touching hers, his hand warm against her midriff. Outside the house the night was calm, the quiet sea ran up on to the beach and fell back with a sigh, a gentle sound like a lullaby.

When would Alex agree to have a baby? She wanted one badly, but whenever she so much as broached the subject he lost his temper. He was successful and wealthy; there was no earthly reason why they shouldn't have children and Sara had somehow expected him to want them. His parents had both died when he was a baby, he never liked to talk about his childhood. He had been placed in an orphanage in London—that much she knew, but there were big gaps in what she had discovered about Alex. She had learnt this much, that when something disturbed him he wouldn't talk about it and if you tried to force him to discuss it he became almost violent.

From their first meeting she had been overpowered by the force of his personality. He had seemed so assured, so dynamic, a glamorous stranger from a world very foreign to her own. Sara had always lived in a little English village, remote from anywhere; she had gone straight from school to work on a small provincial newspaper with a tiny staff, and her experience of life had been strictly limited. Her editor had sent her along to Alex's cottage to try to get an interview with him after Alex had refused to bother with what he saw as an unknown local rag. Cynically, the editor had told Sara to wear her sexiest dress and flutter her eyelashes. 'He likes women,' he had said, but Sara had been far too nervous to make such an obvious play for Alex's attention, and now that she knew him she realised that if she had followed her editor's advice she would have had the door closed in her face.

Instead, she had gone shyly to the cottage, expecting to be turned away, wearing a white denim pants suit, her vivid hair windblown because it was a blustery day and by the time she got to the cottage her neat hairstyle had been wrecked. Alex had listened wryly as she stammered into her reasons for coming, then he had asked her in for a drink. She hadn't dared say much but he had almost dictated the interview to her, amused and sardonic over her obvious lack of experience, and before she left he had asked her to have dinner the next night.

She was incredulous at his interest in her, her parents were disturbed and worried, her friends envious and cynical. When a thirty-three-year-old lone wolf film director with a notorious reputation where women were concerned begins to date an innocent nineteen-year-old girl, the world leaps to obvious conclusions, and Sara's world was no exception. Everyone around her predicted that Alex would lose interest once he had seduced her; none of them expected him to marry her, not even Sara, herself.

Alex had worked with so many beautiful women in the past, dated them, been seen around with them in nightclubs and at parties—Sara couldn't believe at first that he genuinely wanted to marry her. She had said yes because she was crazy about him and out of her head with happiness at the very idea of being his wife, but when she was alone and had time to think, she had inevitably wondered about his motives. Did he want to marry because he wanted children?

She had decided that that must be the reason—Alex, for all his wealth and busy career, had no relatives, no father or mother, brothers or sisters, aunts or uncles. It had seemed unbelievable to Sara when she asked him and was told that he had no family at all; she had thought he must have some relatives somewhere. When she tried to press him further he merely got angry and she learnt to accept what he said on that point without discussion. Alex refused to talk about his past, his life had begun when he got a job as a camera man's assistant in television. He had been seventeen and by the time he was twenty-five he was a television producer of some reputation. His career had advanced by lightning leaps; he moved from television to the cinema and back again to make films intended for both. He worked on both sides of the Atlantic now, freelancing and making only the films he wanted to make.

During the first year of their marriage Sara had waited for him to suggest having a child, but Alex seemed happy to wait. During the second year she had mentioned the idea several times and he had brushed it aside.

He began to get angry whenever she tentatively suggested they talk about having a baby; she would see his black brows jerk together, his golden-brown eyes flash, his mouth tighten in a straight line. Sara was puzzled by his reluctance. She ached to have his child, she brooded over prams in the street and felt incomplete whenever she saw someone with a baby.

She shifted uneasily in the bed and Alex's arm tightened, he touched her bare shoulder with his lips. 'Can't you sleep?' he whispered. 'What's wrong? Does your head hurt?'

'A little,' she said, stretching. She couldn't tell him what she had been thinking about, she didn't want him to get angry again. Sometimes she felt that it had been a mistake for her to give in to Alex so much, she had let him make all the decisions in their life together. She even wore the clothes he liked and read the books he suggested, she had been too young to match the strength of his personality when they met. Alex made the decisions, Sara meekly obeyed him. It wasn't that she wasn't happy with him—she was, deeply happy. Yet some recurring voice inside her kept querying their relationship, disturbing her.

'Do you want some of those pills the doctor gave you?' Alex asked, his body tense.

'No, you know I hate taking pills unless they're absolutely necessary.'

'Do you want the light on?'

She smiled, snuggling closer. 'No, I like the dark.'

His hand softly stroked her relaxed body and she sighed with pleasure. 'That's nice.'

'Is it?' he asked huskily, sliding his hand inside her nightdress and following the smooth tapering line of her thigh.

'Where was I going?' Sara asked, suddenly wondering again. 'On the train this morning— where was I going to?'

'London,' he said shortly. 'Don't try to force your memory, let it come back naturally.' He bit gently the soft, rounded flesh above her arm. 'Try to sleep,' he said, rubbing his face against her back.

'I have tried—I keep thinking and it keeps me awake.'

'I've got a cure for that,' he murmured, the exploration of his hand more daring, inciting her and making her quiver with aroused sensuality. 'Guaranteed—no thinking,' he added, a smile in his voice. She turned carefully on to her back and Alex arched over her, moonlight showing her the pale oval of his face, tumbled black hair around it. He was breathing audibly. 'I want you badly,' he muttered, bending to kiss her in fierce hunger.

Sara ran her arms around his throat and felt his hair brushing her fingertips; the wild strands clinging to her skin, their texture wiry and vital with that electricity Alex seemed to give off with every movement.

'I shouldn't,' she murmured as he lifted his head, leaving her lips hot and faintly bruised.

'Darling, I need you,' he turned and pressed his mouth into the pulsing vein at her wrist, began to kiss the rounded warmth of her bare arm. 'It's been so long,' he groaned, his lips trembling, and Sara frowned in bewilderment. What did he mean by that?

'Have you been away?' she asked uncertainly. Why couldn't she remember? 'Were you working abroad? When did you get back?'

'Don't keep talking,' he said impatiently, the hard angularity of his jaw pressed into her flesh along her shoulder, she felt his lips crawling slowly up her throat, he buried them with a stifled moan in the soft underside of her chin while his hands moved explicitly, intimately, with desire; fondling her breasts, sweeping down her hips, sliding between her thighs. 'Sara,' he whispered, kissing her lips a second later as she tried to ask him where he had been and how long he had been away. Her mood was broken, though; she couldn't relax under his caresses, she felt the jab of worry and uneasiness too much.

'Alex, don't,' she said, turning her head away from his searching mouth. 'I can't think about anything but ... you don't realise how upsetting it is, forgetting months of your life. Talk to me about what happened last week, I may remember then. I know it's June.' She frowned. 'I don't know how I know, but I do. I've remembered Christmas. Why is it always the big events you remember? I can't recall a thing about January. What comes after Christmas? Easter.' She smiled suddenly. 'I remember, you gave me a giant silver egg full of praline chocolates and I took it over to Janie's next day and the children ate all the chocolates. They were all there, Mum and Dad, Robert and James and their wives ... you see, I'm beginning to get it all back. When was Easter? Early April. What happened next? You were at home then. When did you go away?'

He was silent, staring up at the moonlit window, his body rigid and his face a harsh mask, half in the light, half out of it, in an eerie patterning. He rolled away from her and lay down with his back to her.

'It's a mistake to prompt your memory, it will come back bit by bit, the way it's doing now,' he said and his voice was hard and almost rough; she could see that he was struggling with his temper, he was angry because he had wanted to make love and she had rejected him. She had discovered early on in their marriage that Alex became savage if she didn't meet his passion with an equal desire; he was hypersensitive to any form of rebuff, however gentle and temporary. He was possessive without being willing to give himself entirely; he hid so much about himself from her yet insisted on a total submission from Sara which made her entirely his property.

She rarely met his friends, he liked her to stay at the cottage while he was away, working all over the world. Sara hadn't argued about that because she sensed that their life together, in the sea-swept little retreat which was so unlike the other world he inhabited, was his bolt-hole, more important to him than any of the glamour and nervous tension of his career. He frankly admitted he wanted her to himself, he didn't want to share her—and she was too happy about that to worry about the other part of his life, the part into which he would not let her intrude. Even when he was away she had always been in his thoughts; he rang her from New York and South America and France or London. Every night they talked for ten minutes. Alex never told her what he was doing but he asked endless questions about Sara's day, what the weather was like, what flowers were out, what she was reading or listening to on her stereo deck. Alex sent her postcards from all over the world and Sara wrote him long letters giving the minutiae of her life, knowing that was what he wanted to read about, yet, of course, having nothing more exciting to tell him than that she had seen a seal off the rocks below their cottage or that a yacht had been wrecked on the sands a mile away.

Occasionally, it was true, he took her to London for a few days or they flew to the Canaries or the Bahamas for a brief holiday together, but Alex seemed uneasy to see her in those settings. He was happier when they were at the cottage alone; it made Sara happy too, to know that she was all he needed.

'Don't be cross,' she murmured, moving closer to his back.

'I'm not,' Alex said then, and turned to take her back into his arms. 'Go to sleep now,' he whispered and Sara closed her eyes and gradually drifted away into oblivion, safely sheltered in his warm embrace.

When she woke up she was alone in the bed and as she opened her eyes she felt a peculiar dizziness as though something inside her head swung wildly. For a second she grasped at memory, knowing it was only an inch away.

Then she heard her father's voice downstairs and came fully awake, sitting up to listen. He sounded angry, his voice was rising as Sara tried to hear what he was saying. 'You can't do this, Alex! It's dangerous.'

What on earth was he talking about? Sara carefully slid her legs out of the bed and stood on the white carpet. She had a brief giddy sensation for a moment, hearing Alex talking urgently, rapidly, his voice full of insistence but whatever he said pitched too low for her to catch.

'Shocking,' her father said, the one word leaping out of others she didn't catch. She thought he said: 'Very unwise, if not downright unethical,' but what could he mean by that?

Sara walked over to the wardrobe and opened it, the door creaking. She was looking for a robe to wear over her transparent nightie before she went downstairs to see her father. Her hand went automatically to the rail where her clothes hung and she stared in bewilderment seeing nothing but Alex's clothes. Had she recently re-arranged the wardrobe? She opened all the doors, seeing Alex's shirts and jackets, suits and trousers hanging in neat rows. Where were her own clothes?

She heard a door slam downstairs, then the sound of a car engine. Surely her father wasn't leaving without seeing her?

Alex appeared in the doorway and she stared at him, frowning. 'Where are all my clothes? I can't find so much as a pair of panties.'

She saw a flicker of confusion in his eyes, but he pulled himself together quickly. 'What are you doing out of bed? I thought the doctor told you not to get up for two days?' He came towards her with his long-legged stride, that powerful body moving with grace in the casual cotton shirt and old blue denims which she had washed until they were a pale shadow of their original colour. 'Come on, back to bed—I'm just getting your breakfast.' He scooped her into his arms before she could protest and carried her across the room to her bed, depositing her in it gently.

'I heard my father talking, he hasn't gone, has he?' Sara asked, while he pulled a sheet over her.

'I thought you were still asleep, he didn't want to disturb you, he only called in to see how you were.' Alex straightened, raking back a lock of jet black hair. 'How do you feel about kippers for breakfast? You like kippers, don't you?'

'I'll just have some fruit, I think,' she said absently. 'Alex, what has happened to my clothes? I can't understand it—I haven't sent them all the cleaners, now have I?' She laughed uncertainly, her brow furrowed in puzzled distress. There was probably some simple explanation but she wanted to know what it was and Alex was already moving away, she got the feeling he didn't mean to answer her.

'You don't need any clothes, you're staying in that bed,' he said curtly, going out. 'And you can't just have fruit for breakfast, you're ill. I'm having a kipper, I'll bring you one too.'

'Alex!' she called after him but he ran down the stairs without answering. She heard the 'phone ringing then it stopped as Alex picked it up. His voice murmured quietly and Sara stared at the wardrobe, biting her lower lip.

The one possibility she could come up with was that she and Alex had quarrelled recently and she had moved out of their bedroom into one of the other two rooms. That would explain why Alex had said last night that it was a long time since they made love, it would explain the odd silences and tensions she had been so puzzled by yesterday.

Her skin suddenly went cold. She had a memory of packing; clothes everywhere in the bedroom, shoes piled on the floor, cases standing around her, half full. She closed her eyes, trying to concentrate. Where had she been going? Her eyes stung as if she was going to cry. She had been crying that day, her hands shaking as she flung clothes into the cases. Had Alex been there?

She searched in the shadowy recesses of her

mind but as suddenly as the memory had surfaced, it had sunk again, leaving her with nothing but a certainty that she had recently packed all her clothes to go somewhere and that she had been very unhappy.

When the train crashed she had had only a small suitcase with her—or had there been other cases which had gone on to London without anyone realising that they were hers? She might have stacked them in the corridor, she decided. They would all have her address on them, Alex had a range of matching luggage which had plastic-covered address labels tagged on the handle. Sooner or later, the cases would be discovered and returned to her, but why wouldn't Alex tell her where she had been going and why?

He came up the stairs a second later and carried a tray towards her. The smoked fish smelt delicious, after all, and Sara suddenly felt hungry. Alex laid the tray on her knees and piled pillows behind her head.

'I'll be bored if I have to stay in bed all day,' she said, watching him. The sunlight turned his brown skin to polished bronze, he looked faintly Red Indian, with those sculptured bones and deep eye sockets, his black hair brushed back off his bony forehead. She was never quite sure what gave him such a primitive air; perhaps it was those untamed eyes, gleaming and predatory, or the creature lurking behind them out of sight, secret and unreachable, the Alex she did not know and who had grown up without human ties or love, like some wild animal which flees at the first approach.

'Doctor's orders,' he said. 'Eat your breakfast before it gets cold.'

'Can I have something to read? A newspaper?'

'I haven't been down to get one for a couple of days.'

'Can I have the radio then?' she pleaded, smiling at him as she picked up the glass of freshly squeezed orange.

'Radio,' he said, as though thinking about the request, then said: 'I've got a great detective story you'd enjoy—I'll get that for you, you always enjoy good detective stories.'

'I'll have the radio, too,' she called as he left. 'I can listen to music while I read.'

'I'll bring the record player up with a stack of records,' he said, from the stairs, his voice final.

She enjoyed the kipper, which was tender and delicately flavoured, and drank two cups of the coffee. Alex hadn't made it strong, she noted, smiling, perhaps because he thought she shouldn't drink strong coffee with a head injury. In all the years of their marriage she could never remember him being so solicitous and watchful of her. Alex rarely entered the kitchen although he was quite capable of cooking a meal.

She heard the 'phone ringing again and Alex's impatient footsteps as he went to answer it. It wasn't unusual for him to get an endless succession of 'phone calls. Sometimes he told her to say he was out; it irked him to spend hours talking on the 'phone.

She bent down to place the tray on the floor and as she straightened again her forehead throbbed fiercely and she lay back, eyes closed, wincing. The stitches were pulling, the pain quite sharp. She shouldn't have bent down so suddenly.

When Alex came back with a portable record player he stopped in his tracks, staring at her. 'What's wrong?' His voice was tense, on edge, and Sara opened her eyes, hurriedly dragging a smile into her face.

'I'm just resting as ordered,' she lied because he looked so worried that she didn't want to tell him how dizzy she felt.

He relaxed and arranged the record player on a small table next to her bed then went off to find some records and the book he had promised her. Under his arm he had a pile of scripts in broad yellow covers. He handed her the detective story, dropping the scripts on the pink velvet armchair by the window.

'Are you going to stay up here with me?' Sara asked hopefully and he looked round, his hard mouth curving into a smile.

'Don't you want me?' The question meant far more than the surface words and Sara laughed, eying him back with mockery.

'I'll consider it. Is there a Billy Joel LP there or . . .'

Alex produced a Billy Joel record and put that on the record player, then he settled down in the chair with his scripts, his slim body lounging casually, long legs crossed at the knee, his head thrown back against the velvet cushions. Sara had redecorated this room after they were married; it had been a rather bare place before that and she had bought the pink velvet chair and the white carpet with the money her parents had given her as a wedding present. She had hung the wallpaper with its delicate pink roses and green leaves, painted the white woodwork, decided where the carpenter should fit the wardrobes and sewn the curtains on her new electric sewing machine. For the first two years of their marriage Sara had been totally engrossed in turning Alex's spartan, sparsely furnished weekend retreat into a comfortable home for both of them. She hadn't hurried, doing one room at a time, whenever Alex was away it had filled her days and occupied her attention. It was only when the whole cottage was exactly the way she wanted it that she began to feel restless.

She concentrated on her book, becoming interested in the storyline, and whenever her mind wandered briefly she had a pleasurable sense of peace, the room was quiet, the sunlight warm without being uncomfortable, Alex was making his way through the scripts with his usual speed. Sara liked having him there, working a few feet away from her. He always got piles of scripts to consider, they seemed to come by every post, and they almost always went back again once Alex had gutted them, his mouth hard and impatient. He had a technique of reading fast; running an eye down the page, tasting the style and structure rapidly. If he was vaguely interested he would then start from the beginning and read until his attention was lost when he would drop the discarded script on to a pile on the floor beside his chair, picking up the next one.

Sara was nearly halfway through her book

when Alex gave a sigh and got up, gathering up the pile of scripts.

'No good?' Sara asked, looking up.

He shrugged. 'An average bunch—nothing spectacular.' He went to change the record again—he had changed it several times that morning, and Sara was tired of listening to music.

'Don't put another one on,' she said quickly and he turned off the machine and smiled at her.

'What do you want for lunch?'

'Salad? Have you got any?' She stopped short on that question, stiffening, as memory stabbed again, even more elusive than before. It wasn't so much that she remembered a particular event, as that she had asked him that question in a tone that disturbed her although she couldn't say why. Was it because the question implied that she had no idea what Alex had in the kitchen? She shivered, feeling excluded, shut out, which was absurd in this sunlit room with Alex standing so close and watching her with alert, attentive eyes.

'What is it?' he asked in that voice she was beginning to recognise. Alex knew at once that something was wrong.

'I feel cold,' she said childishly and he came over and sank down on the bed, putting his arms around her.

'Does your head hurt?' He sounded even more anxious and Sara clung, her face against his throat.

'I'm so frightened—why can't I remember? I feel like a freak.'

He stroked her hair gently. 'Don't be silly, you're not a freak—you're beautiful and I love you.' His hand moved down her back, warm and possessive, gripping her closer. She felt his mouth searching for her lips and as she gave them to him Alex gently pushed her down against the pillows and kissed her with a heated intensity that made her tremble. She wound her arms round him and arched in helpless response, needing his passion to drive back the atavistic fear of the darkness which had trapped her a few minutes earlier. While she was held in his arms she was safe, that terrifying blankness couldn't snatch her away.

She had a painful sinking suspicion that when she remembered everything she had forgotten, she was going to be unhappy—she didn't know why she suspected that, only that increasingly she felt miserable whenever her memory seemed to be on the point of returning. She felt as though that lost memory was dammed up somewhere inside her head, and when the dam broke and the waters flooded out she might drown, and Alex might not be there to save her. It was crazy thinking, Alex wouldn't let anything happen to her—what could ever separate the two of them?

'Don't ever let me go!' she whispered, clinging to him.

'Never,' Alex said harshly and for a second the silence seemed tense with a feeling Sara trembled at—a silence shattered by the sound of a car engine. Alex lifted his head, listening, his body rigid. The car slowed and stopped right outside.

'My parents, I expect,' Sara said shakily, smiling, but before she had got to the end of that remark Alex had broken away from her, sprung to his feet and glanced out of the window. The next second he was racing out of the room without another word, and Sara was startled. His face had been stiff and pale, set in what could almost be described as shock and had certainly been rage. Surely he didn't object to her seeing her parents? The idea was ludicrous, yet why had he been quarrelling with her father earlier that day? Why had her father gone without coming up to see her?

Stumbling out of the bed she got to the window and leant on the sill to look down. It was not her father's car she saw; it was a small, rakish white sports car, and the driver was just sliding her long legs out of the driver's seat. Sara couldn't see her face, only the top of her pale blonde head, but she recognised the woman immediately. She took a deep, harsh breath, staring; the dam broke and the waters of memory poured through her head.

CHAPTER FOUR

THROUGH the painful, bewildering, intolerable rush of memories she heard Alex saying angrily: 'What the hell are *you* doing here?' Swaying backwards, Sara sat down on the arm of the chair he had been sitting in all morning, the velvet warm from the sun. She gripped the back of the chair and tried to hear the woman's voice, cold perspiration breaking out on her skin as she recognised it.

'I brought an important script that LJ wants you to read at once, he's sure this is the one you've been looking for,' the cool voice drawled.

Sara had felt uneasy the first time she ever set eyes on Madeleine Bentley. The other woman was so different from herself, in many ways her opposite and the type of woman Sara would have expected Alex to find attractive—sophisticated, elegant, ultra sure of herself. Madeleine had been working for Alex for several months before Sara actually met her in person. Sara had heard her voice on the 'phone many times before that. Cool, assured, edged with a note which was impossible to pin down but which made Sara's hackles rise, the voice had seemed to hint at amused contempt whenever Sara shyly answered the 'phone. Sara couldn't explain that it made her jump when the 'phone rang unexpectedly or tell the unseen woman that she hated it when Alex's other world broke in upon the halcyon peace of their life together in the cottage. Sara had a young, unsophisticated voice and a hesitant manner when she was dealing with her husband's important contacts. His secretary hadn't bothered to hide the fact that she despised the wife Alex kept hidden away.

Looking back now she wondered if some female intuition had warned her from the beginning that Madeleine was a threat to her?

'Why didn't he just post it?' Alex snapped and Madeleine laughed, the light silvery sound setting Sara's teeth on edge. She had never hated anyone in her life until the day she discovered that her husband was having an affair with Madeleine Bentley. The ferocity of her own reaction to that had shocked her; she hadn't thought herself capable of such a deep and violent emotion. Her love for Alex hadn't had that piercing depth, it had been too uncertain and tremulous and Alex had made her so happy that the lance of pain had never entered their relationship until it was made clear that she had lost him.

'You know LJ. He always wants instant decisions,' Madeleine said drily. 'This script arrived on Friday and he took it home with him to read. Sandy and Pol wrote it, he hoped it would be good. He had one of his famous flashes of intuition about it and now that he's actually read it he's very excited. He wants to buy it but he needs your reaction first—he says you're the only director who could handle the material with enough subtlety.'

'Oh, very well, give it to me,' Alex said in a flat voice. Sara couldn't see either of them now that she was sitting down, her head was below the level of the window sill, but she could hear them quite clearly, their voices rising through the warm summer air.

She was listening and thinking at one and the same time; realising so many things at once that her mind was like a minefield into which some unwary innocent has wandered; crashes and explosions of blinding light were going off all around her. She wasn't thinking clearly, she couldn't keep up with all the new data being processed, her anger kept stabbing at her, her lips moved in silent fury, unheard exclamations she suppressed in case the two outside heard her. She wanted to hear what they said, not let them hear what she was thinking.

How soon had Alex realised that her head wound had left her with amnesia? Long before she innocently told him, expecting him to be surprised and taken aback—that was obvious now. Alex had known, perhaps from the minute he walked into that waiting-room and she held out her arms to him, so openly relieved and delighted to see him. He hadn't blinked, the bastard. He had seen his opportunity and with typical, ruthless, cool-headed quick wit had seized it—and her.

She hadn't forgotten a few weeks of her life—she had lost more than a year, her mind like a wiped computer tape from which vital bits of information are missing, and Alex had taken advantage of that. Pictures formed like bubbles in some cartoon, floating around her head—images of herself in his arms, kissing him, clinging to him while that opportunistic swine made love to her and tried to . . .

She hissed, stifling the sound with one hand over her own mouth. They must not hear her. What had he kept on saying this morning? Don't try to force your memory, darling, don't try to remember, my love . . .

She bit her knuckles, her blood boiling, needing to do something violent. But why to yourself, you dummy? she asked. Why not to him? Kill him, she thought with yearning, yes that would make her feel better, she would enjoy that. Shoot him, stab him through that black heart, strangle him, poison him? How many ways were there to kill someone? None that were slow enough, she wanted to watch him die inch by inch by some long-drawn out torture.

Madeleine was laughing outside. Damn her, thought Sara, damn both of them. 'You don't sound wild with enthusiasm,' Madeleine was saying.

'I'm up to here in scripts,' Alex said. 'I can't get worked up over yet another of them, I've read too many today.' He sounded brusque, abstracted, and no doubt he was trying to think fast. He must be wondering how to get rid of Madeleine before Sara saw her and began to remember. He was probably keeping one eye on the bedroom window, hoping that Sara hadn't thought of getting out of bed to see who had arrived, hoping she couldn't hear their voices. Alex was a quick thinker—he thought on his feet, like a good boxer, seeing the punches coming and ducking and weaving out of trouble long before they could connect. Wasn't that why he had been so swift to see his opportunity when he realised that Sara had forgotten everything that had happened over the past year?

How could he do it? Sara thought again, the question recurring with disbelieving outrage every time she stopped remembering and started reacting. He knew she hated him, knew she had very good reason to hate him, yet he had coolly seized that unexpected opportunity to get her into bed again; it was despicable. If Madeleine knew . . .

She sat very still, her face startled by that idea. Of course—Alex was playing a very dangerous game, wasn't he? It wasn't simply that he did not want Sara to see Madeleine; he couldn't want Madeleine to see Sara, either. His clever little game had backfired on him in a way he hadn't expected. How would that corkscrew mind of his get him out of this?

'Aren't you going to ask me in for a drink, darling?' Madeleine asked.

Sara stiffened, listening.

'I've driven eighty miles to get here,' Madeleine added, laughing. 'I sometimes wish LJ wasn't quite so insistent on instant reactions. I'd no sooner got into work this morning than he was thrusting that script into my hands and telling me to get it to you today without fail.'

'You should have sent a courier,' Alex said shortly.

'It seemed a better idea to come myself,' Madeleine said drily. 'Obviously I was wrong. Is my arrival inconvenient, darling?'

Sara's mouth twisted angrily—you bet it is, she thought, waiting to hear Alex's answer to that, and then, suddenly, asked herself: why am I hiding, cowering out of sight as though I was guilty of something? What have I done? Except lose my memory and fall prey to that sneaky two-timing swine out there?

'I'm sorry, Madeleine, but I have a lot of work to do and I can't spare the time to entertain visitors,' Alex said. 'I came down here for some peace and quiet.'

Sara got up and leaned on the window sill. They were still standing at the gate; Alex blocking the path and Madeleine Bentley facing him, the sunlight giving her blonde head the lustre of a halo which was totally inappropriate for the woman wearing it. Sara's hostile eyes ran over the chic outfit she was also wearing; very Mayfair silk shirt with classy pearls around her throat and pearl studs in her ear lobes, a smooth skirt which cut off around her knees showing a good deal of her long, shapely legs. She didn't fit these surroundings, she was too glossy.

'You're in one of your inhospitable moods, are you?' Madeleine asked, looking discontented, as well she might, having driven all this way expecting to be welcomed with open arms— literally, no doubt, Sara added viciously.

They hadn't realised they were under observation. She meant to remedy that immediately. She opened the window, leaning out.

Madeleine's eyes shot upwards, rounding like great blue saucers. Alex spun as if she had shot him in the back—and she wished she had.

She did not, however, let Madeleine see that. That was no part of Sara's new game plan. Smiling limpidly, with no visible trace of the emotions raging inside her, she said: 'Are you going to be long, darling? I'm waiting for you, remember.'

It would have been difficult to say whose expression was the most stupefied—both of them stared up at her, jaws dropping, mouths wide open, struck dumb. But Alex had at least the advantage of knowing that she was in the cottage before she appeared at the window. Madeleine's eyes were incredulous—and very busy. They skated over her tousled hair, bare arms and shoulders, the warm flesh of her breasts revealed by the deep cleavage of her lace and silk nightie. Madeleine noticed every detail and didn't like what she saw. Sara found the other woman's unhidden reaction distinctly comforting; she wasn't petty enough to want revenge but she couldn't help feeling that that was what she was getting. The acid irony of the situation would probably seem funny to her when she wasn't quite so angry with Alex—even at that moment she could get a twisted sort of amusement out of it. Alex didn't seem to find it in the least funny, of course—which made it better.

It couldn't be every day that an ex-wife was caught *in flagrante delicto* with her ex-husband, by the mistress who had initially caused their marriage to break down. There ought, Sara considered coolly, to be a good script in there somewhere—if she didn't feed Alex a slow poison within the next hour or so she might point that out to him as a farewell present.

'Well,' Madeleine finally said, getting her breath and her voice back. 'Hallo.'

Sara ignored her. She wasn't wasting time on Madeleine. 'Hurry back, darling,' she purred in Alex's direction and left the window without so much as looking at Madeleine again.

'When did that happen?' Madeleine said to Alex. 'You're very secretive—I thought your divorce was almost final, the last I heard . . .'

'I have to go,' Alex said curtly, interrupting the clipped words. Sara heard his footsteps followed by the slam of the front door, then after a pause the even more violent slam of Madeleine's car door and the roar of her engine. She drove away, accelerating much too fast with a screech of tyres, just as Alex walked into the bedroom.

Sara had got back into bed. She didn't intend to stay there long but she had to get her breath back and her act together; she couldn't quite make up her mind what to do to him. She stared fixedly at him, her head chaotic with ideas of violence which made her shake, and Alex registered her expression with wary assessment.

Sara opened her mouth a fraction, her teeth almost clenched. Through that tiny slit she hissed: 'You bastard. You conniving, cheating bastard.' She had so much more to say on that line that the words jammed up inside her and she fizzed like a shaken bottle of champagne, ready to explode with a bang.

Alex didn't come any closer, he was far too cute for that. He stayed out of range of anything she might throw at him, out of arm's length in case she tried to hit him, and she could see from his expression that he was trying to out-think her, planning his strategy on the run.

'How could you do such a despicable thing?' she asked without expecting a reply because what possible excuse could he give? 'How could anyone pull such a dirty trick?' she continued, her rhetoric warming up. 'What sort of low down rat would even think of it?' she asked the middle of his stomach, refusing to look at his face. 'Opportunistic, sneaky, contemptible . . .' She hadn't run out of adjectives but there were so many to choose from that she paused to pick the most incisive, and Alex moved across the room, sideways, like a crab, scuttling to the far end of the bed. 'Devious, lying, amoral, unscrupulous,' Sara continued without repeating herself once. She didn't need to—Alex had every fault in the book and she meant to catalogue them one by one.

'What else could I have done?' he asked her coolly and she couldn't believe her ears, staring at him in furious disbelief. Alex sat down on the edge of the bed but his eyes were still wary, he was watching her intently and poised to duck out of the way if she threw something at him.

'What else?' she snarled. 'Of all the . . .'

'When I arrived at the hospital and realised you had amnesia I couldn't very well break it to you that we'd split up—I didn't know what effect that might have. You were obviously disturbed and off balance, being told that we were in the middle of getting divorced might have been disastrous. I had to play along, try to reassure you.'

Sara was speechless—he was using a blandly reasonable voice, trying to sell her this image of himself as a kindly man doing his best in a difficult situation, turning the truth on its head, his eyes reproachful.

Her lip curled. 'And is that why you tried to seduce me?' Her voice vibrated with the bitter anger she felt about that and she couldn't halt the hot flow of colour rushing up to her hairline. Alex had made insistent love to her ever since they arrived back at the cottage; she had escaped sleeping with him by the skin of her teeth—or, more accurately, she had escaped having sex with him, because, of course, she had in fact slept in the same bed. Her eyes hated him but Alex met their accusation without flinching.

'I didn't have to try very hard,' he murmured and her scalp almost lifted as her rage pushed against it.

'You . . . you . . . bastard,' she stammered, but she had called him that and the husky word seemed too tame for what she wanted to say.

'You obviously thought we were still happily married—I thought it would seem odd to you if I didn't so much as kiss you. I was following my instincts.'

She seethed, staring at him. 'Your instincts?' she repeated scathingly. 'Yes, I know all about those—the instincts of the alley cat!'

He didn't like that, although he tried to hide

his anger by lowering his lashes over those
suddenly stiletto-sharp eyes. Sara felt a brief
satisfaction; she had managed to get one arrow
through the plated steel of his armour, it wasn't
quite enough for her but it was at least one tiny
victory.

'Did you tell my parents that I had amnesia?'
she asked, thinking back.

'Of course,' he said coolly. 'Why should I try
to hide it from them? I explained what I was
doing and they understood.'

'Liar,' she said hoarsely. 'I heard my father
talking to you, I didn't realise what was going on
at the time but it's all too crystal clear now! He
was objecting to your trickery, wasn't he?
Shocking, he said—what you were doing was
shocking, that was what he meant, wasn't it? My
father didn't like it, he called you unethical, and
he was understating the case—you probably
haven't even got the word ethical in your
dictionary. I don't know how you managed to
keep him away from me, you must have talked
fast, what lies did you tell him to convince him
that he shouldn't interfere?'

'I told him you still loved me,' Alex told her;
so calmly and in such a level tone that for a
second or two she didn't take it in, staring at
him.

Then she went red, a burning, scalded red that
drained out of her face as fast as it had come,
leaving her white and cold-skinned.

'I *hate* you,' she said with a depth that made
her voice harsh.

His eyes flickered, the pupils black and hard,

dilating with what might be shock or merely anger; the brown skin drawn tensely over his cheekbones, his mouth a straight, forceful line, his jaw set grimly. For a moment he stared at her and Sara threw back her head in bitter defiance, projecting towards him all the raw hostility she felt for him. He wasn't getting away with a statement like that. Love him? Once, when she was young and blind and a fool—but not now, never again, her eyes were open and she knew too much about him.

Alex was the first to recover. She watched him pull himself together, those leonine eyes glowing, bright gold with insistence. He wasn't a man who accepted setbacks, who admitted defeat, he was too much of a fighter—that was why she had refused to see him during the past year. She had known the dangers of a personal confrontation.

'You have an unusual way of showing hate,' he said with mockery, his eyes reminding her, silently drawing pictures which made her spine stiffen.

'I'd forgotten,' she said tersely. Amnesia had wiped out all the lessons she had learnt over the past year, stripped her of the defences which she had built up while they were apart. She had become vulnerable again, overnight, running back into his arms like a child that has forgotten fire can burn. The amnesia had placed her in Alex's power and he hadn't been slow to see his advantage and take it.

He was smiling derisively and she eyed him back, wishing she could wipe that look off his face.

'Or you'd remembered,' Alex drawled, the hardness of his mouth curving in mocking sensuality. 'That's the real truth, isn't it? You've always been mine however much you tried to convince yourself otherwise. You didn't forget, you let yourself remember—there's a big difference.'

'Oh, you think you're so clever, don't you?' Sara gabbled incoherently, biting back a scream of pure rage at his amused expression. 'You didn't want me to remember, don't think I haven't realised that. That was the last thing you wanted—you did everything you could think of to stop me remembering. Ever since we got back here, you've been telling me not to worry, not to ask questions you found inconvenient, questions which might just have prodded my memory about things you'd prefer me to forget.' She leaned forward, her face contemptuous, imitating his voice: 'Don't try to remember, darling,' she mimicked. 'Don't fret your little head about it.'

'I told you that you'd remember naturally and I was right, wasn't I?' Alex countered without hesitation.

'I remembered because I saw your mistress out there,' Sara yelled. 'It must have been a nasty shock for you when she showed up, that wasn't part of your plan, was it?'

'She is *not* my mistress,' Alex said at once, frowning and looking grim, the black slash of his brows giving his golden eyes more emphasis. She wasn't surprised to hear him deny it; he had denied it a year ago when Sara first discovered what had been going on behind her back. He had gone on denying it but then it was typical of him not to know when he was found out, when the horse had bolted and it was pointless to pretend to lock the stable door.

She gave him a sarcastic, barbed smile. 'I'd never heard that amnesia was catching—I must talk to my doctor about this, medical science may still have a lot to learn.'

'*You* have a lot to learn!' Alex said shortly and she didn't like the way he was staring at her, it sent a frisson of uneasiness down her spine.

'Not from you,' she muttered, which was a psychological mistake, but she realised that too late as he gave her a brooding, menacing smile, nodding.

'Oh, yes, Sara.' He got up and she tensed against the pillows, shrinking away.

'Don't you come near me or . . .'

'Or what?' he asked softly, prowling towards her, the graceful lope of his body all threat.

'Get out of here,' she yelled. 'I'm getting dressed and then I'm ringing my father to come and get me and take me home.'

'Getting dressed in what?' Alex asked tauntingly and Sara looked into his gleaming eyes with suspicion.

'My clothes—where are they?' Her glance flicked around the room. 'Where are my clothes? What have you done with them?' She couldn't see them anywhere and she sensed from his expression that they were no longer in this room, he had taken them away, hidden them.

'You aren't going anywhere,' Alex assured her. 'You don't need your clothes because you're staying in that bed.' He sat down on the edge of it, far too close to her, blandly smiling. 'I promised the hospital that you wouldn't get up for at least two days. We can't have you running the risk of bursting those stitches in your head, can we? Your amnesia might come back, you wouldn't want that.'

'You're not doing this to me,' Sara promised, shaking with temper, very flushed and agitated.

He smiled again and she hated the way he smiled, she was tense under the lazy inspection of his wandering eyes, the way they lingered on the deep neckline of her nightdress. She had been puzzled by her own sensual awareness of him ever since he collected her at the hospital; that should have warned her, but of course she hadn't had any idea that the reason why his sidelong glances and seductive hands made her tremble was because it was over a year since he had made love to her. Looking away, her face cold, she pulled the sheet up to her chin now to hide the shadowy cleft between her half-bared breasts, the vulnerable pallor of her throat, the naked curve of her shoulders.

Alex laughed at her, his eyes bright and teasing. 'What are you hiding? Nothing I haven't seen hundreds of times.' He leaned forward and she thought he was going to drag the sheet away from her, but he looked into her nervous green eyes, his face amused. 'Seen, and touched,' he whispered. 'And kissed,' he added, his voice silky, tormenting. 'If it gives you the delusion that you're safe, cover yourself from head to toe, Sara—it won't make any difference. You're mine and when I want you I'll take you—and there's nothing you can do to stop me, nothing you'll even want to do to stop me.'

'You kid yourself,' she said in a thin, thready voice she tried to make convincing. She didn't succeed, she knew that from the mockery in his eyes.

'A few hours ago I practically had to fight you off,' he said and she burned with shame and embarrassment because she couldn't deny it, only deny that she had known what she knew now, only defend herself by saying that she had forgotten that they were no longer married, and that was a very weak defence. Her mind might reject Alex but her body had other ideas, and now he knew it, and he wouldn't scruple to use that knowledge.

'Get out of my room,' she said harshly.

'Our room,' he corrected.

'Mine,' she insisted.

'We shared it last night,' he murmured and she flinched at the feline mockery in his gaze; he had her trapped and was flexing his claws before using them on her, he had no intention of letting her escape. Alex hadn't had enough fun out of his game yet. Sara's eyes stung with a desperation and bitterness she only just fought down. She had betrayed herself into his hands and Alex was enjoying her tormented inability to get away.

'I want to talk to my father,' she said, getting out of bed.

'I've had the 'phone disconnected,' Alex said complacently and she stood very still, shaking her head, refusing to believe him.

'I heard it ring all morning, don't lie to me!'

'It hasn't rung for hours,' he said coolly. 'I asked the telephone company to disconnect it until further notice. I told them I had a very sick person in the house who mustn't be disturbed.' He smiled lazily at her. 'They were very understanding and sympathetic.'

'I don't believe you,' Sara said desperately, but she did—he was far too calm for it to be a lie.

'Go ahead, find out for yourself,' Alex said, leaning against the window sill and watching her as she hesitated. She looked almost dazedly around the room, panic beating inside her as though a wild bird was fluttering against her rib cage. She was helplessly in his power here, she couldn't escape in this flimsy nightdress and there were no neighbours but the gulls and an occasional visiting seal. The cottage was isolated, had no telephone now, was miles from the village and rarely saw any cars because people preferred to use the other road. What was she going to do?

CHAPTER FIVE

SHE swayed, faintly dizzy, and Alex moved away from the window hurriedly. He put his arm round her and supported her body with his own. Sara slapped his hands away.

'Let go of me!'

'Get back into bed, you're in no condition to be on your feet,' he said in a brusque voice, and she reacted to that tone by stepping back too fast. Her head spun and Alex made a smothered growling sound, steering her back towards the bed. She didn't have the strength to argue any more, she collapsed against the pillows, her eyes closed. The room was going round and round, it made her feel sick to watch it.

'Sara?' Alex's voice seemed to come from a long, long way off. It sounded worried, and she hoped he *was* beginning to worry. He had had no business to bring her here, isolate her from medical help, keep her memory lapse a secret. She had been a fool not to tell the doctor at the hospital, but then she hadn't realised how serious her amnesia really was—she had imagined she had lost a few days, it hadn't dawned on her that she had lost over a year of her life.

'Go away,' she mouthed at him without opening her eyes, not even certain her words were audible. If they were, she couldn't hear them; her ears were buzzing with hypertension, she was almost deaf, she felt like someone flying in a plane whose air pressure has gone haywire.

'Drink this,' Alex said, lifting her head and putting a glass of cold water to her lips. She sipped reluctantly, keeping her eyes closed. She was afraid to open them in case the vertigo returned, it had been a terrifying experience.

Alex lowered her head and drew the covers over her. 'Lie still and try to sleep,' he said.

She ignored him. Pretending that he wasn't there didn't make him disappear but it made it easier to bear his presence. Was it the shock of remembering—or the shock of seeing Madeleine again—that had made her feel so ill? Both, probably, she realised grimly. They were, after all, inextricably entwined, an obvious chain of cause and effect. Who knew how long she might have had the amnesia if Madeleine hadn't come down to the cottage with that script? Madeleine obviously still worked for Alex and that was another proof that he had lied because if they hadn't had an affair surely she wouldn't still be working for him? The fact that Madeleine was still in his life was a tacit admission of their relationship.

Sara had been quite friendly with the secretary who had been working for Alex when Sara married him. Rosalie had been a down-to-earth woman of thirty-five who had unexpectedly become pregnant after deciding she would never be able to have children. She had resigned to enjoy her baby without the pressure of such a hectic job, and Sara had thought, then, that one day soon she would have a baby, too. She had kept in touch with Rosalie for a while until the little family moved to Leeds.

Sara had hoped she would make friends with Madeleine at first, but that was before she talked to her and heard the off hand mockery, the sneering disdain with which Madeleine spoke every time she rang Alex at the cottage and got Sara first.

Madeleine disliked and despised her and didn't bother to hide the fact. She had no time for her own sex. She was a man's woman; ambitious, tough-minded, clever and very sophisticated. She and Sara had had nothing in common except Alex—and although Sara had been so blindly unaware of it for a long time, Alex had been more of a bone of contention between them than a link.

Sara realised now that Madeleine was more Alex's kind of woman—they had similar minds, the same attitudes. They were both creatures of the jungle; predatory, dangerous. It didn't really surprise her to discover that Madeleine wanted Alex—although it almost destroyed her to find out that Alex wanted Madeleine. She knew she had no weapons to use against a woman like that, she couldn't compete on equal terms with that glittering sexuality.

Her own femininity was of a very different kind; warm, loving, gentle. She had allowed Alex to dictate the terms of their marriage; he had always been the stronger personality, the dominant one, and she had blissfully believed that by yielding to him, giving him everything he wanted, she made him happy. She had been bitterly disillusioned.

She might never have found out about their affair if Madeleine's husband had not made sure she was told. He had come down to the cottage one day with a large brown envelope stuffed with the evidence his private detective had uncovered—dates and places where the lovers had met, furtively taken snapshots of them in hotel rooms together, an unfinished love letter to Alex from Madeleine which had first warned her husband that she was having an affair with her boss, the evidence of hotel staff who had seen them together in a room at night. Madeleine had calmly admitted the affair, said she was in love with Alex, wanted to marry him. The divorce was to be uncontested.

The day Matt Bentley came to see her, though, his divorce case hadn't yet reached the courts. It was the first Sara had heard of it and she had turned white as she listened.

He had looked at her defiantly. 'I had to tell you,' he said. 'You'll have to know, sooner or later, I've no doubt your husband will ask you for a divorce so that he can marry Madeleine.' Then he had muttered: 'I'm sorry,' as though he was embarrassed by the pain in her eyes.

Sara had felt a flash of intuition, her mouth cold and sardonic. 'You're telling me to get your revenge on Alex,' she had guessed and watched the man redden.

'Why should he get away with it?' he had broken out, tacitly admitting the motive.

Afterwards Sara had wondered what twisted pleasure he had got out of telling her, watching her suffer the way he must have suffered when he found out. During those first weeks after his visit she had changed inch by inch, day by day, as the poison he had injected into her sank into her nature. She had begun to doubt, to suspect, to hate—she had experienced new sensations; cynicism, despair, distaste. She had always been a very happy woman, she was not prepared for humiliation and grief.

Alex had denied it, of course. His affair with Madeleine had not, apparently, been as serious as her husband believed. Matt Bentley had blamed Alex, believed that Madeleine had been seduced and tempted by high living and expensive presents. He claimed his marriage had been happy until Alex broke it up, but right from the first Sara hadn't believed that part of his story. She knew Madeleine a little better than that.

Matt Bentley was a well-dressed, attractive man with a smooth manner, but he was only a travelling salesman with a firm of drug manufacturers. He might have seemed a good catch to Madeleine when they first met, but not any more. She had seen another life style, she had mixed with the high and the mighty, and she thought she could get something better than Matt Bentley. She had traded him in like a discarded car, last year's model, already out of date.

Sara hadn't thought like that then—as she looked at Matt Bentley she had only wished he would go so that she could cry in private. The first appalling blow hadn't worn off, she hadn't quite realised all it meant. Shock waves of emotion had broken over her head for days afterwards, but at first she had only felt a peculiar mixture of numbed disbelief and fear, like someone who has had a limb amputated and is still anaesthetised by shock. The real agony had begun long afterwards.

Alex had denied the whole story when she faced him with what Matt Bentley had told her. He had been oddly wary the minute she began to speak, though.

'It isn't true,' he had said at once, too quickly.

'Are they getting divorced?' Sara had asked in a dry, flat voice.

'Yes, but . . .'

'And he is claiming she committed adultery with you?' she had interrupted, her voice still unfamiliar, suddenly adult, unrecognisably hard.

'It's all lies,' he had said.

'Mr Bentley told me that his wife had admitted it,' Sara had accused and seen the uncertain flicker of Alex's eyes, guessed that he was hurriedly trying to think up some story to explain that. She realised at that moment that Alex hadn't intended to change a thing in his life—he had wanted to have his cake and eat it, keep Sara as his wife, back at the cottage, discreetly separated from his busy jetsetting life on the film circuit, while he continued with his more glamorous affair with Madeleine behind the scenes. Alex didn't want a divorce. He had it made—wife and mistress, a cosy combination for any man.

'If you love me, you'll trust me,' Alex had said and she had been dumbfounded.

'If I love you?' she had repeated incredulously. 'If I love you? I tell you that I've been shown evidence like that, and you ask me to forget all about it and trust you?'

'If you love me, prove it,' Alex had said with a stubborn stare and she had become so angry she trembled with rage.

'Tell me, I'm curious,' she had asked fiercely. 'How does it turn out to be me who's on trial here? Don't I deserve an explanation? You can't seriously expect . . .'

'I expect you to take my word for it that I haven't had an affair with anyone. It's up to you whether you believe me or not—if you love me, you won't ask any more questions.'

'Just like that?' She had looked at him and wondered if she had ever known him. She couldn't believe that it was happening, that he was merely brushing the matter aside and insisting that she accept his word without further explanation, and yet she should have been prepared for that moment by everything that had gone before.

It wasn't the first time that Alex had over-ridden her queries, her own wishes, forced her to accept his way of life without question. Sara had almost begged him to have a child and he had told her it was impossible. At first she had thought that he meant that he couldn't have children, but that had not been the reason—Alex simply didn't want children, he got angry if she mentioned the idea. He knew how much she wanted a baby, but it would take up too much of her attention, Alex didn't care if it made her unhappy or if she was lonely when he was away for weeks on end. The matter was closed, he said. No children. Sara must not mention it again.

He wouldn't let her get a job, either, even a part-time job to keep her occupied while he was away. Alex's life was busy and fulfilled, he didn't allow Sara as much, and now he was insisting that she turn a blind eye to his affair with his secretary!

'If you love me,' she had said stiffly, 'you'll explain what is going on between you and Madeleine, if it isn't an affair.'

'For God's sake!' Alex had exploded. 'Will you drop the subject? I'm not her lover, I have no plans to be her lover, her divorce is nothing to do with me.'

'So her husband is lying? He made the whole thing up?'

Alex had looked at her with a scowl pulling his black brows together, for a second she had thought he was going to answer her, then he had turned on his heel and walked out, slamming the door.

Sara hadn't believed her marriage could end so quickly. She stood there listening to the echo of that slamming door and couldn't believe her ears. Alex had gone out, she had gone upstairs and packed some clothes and then she had rung her father and asked him to drive over to pick her up. Her parents had been shattered, they had tried to persuade her to go back, to talk to Alex—and when she refused, had begged her at least to see him in their home and talk to him there. Sara wouldn't even listen to them. She made her father drive her to the station and caught a train to London to stay with an old school friend who had married and gone to the capital to live and work.

Penelope had been welcoming and discreet, she hadn't asked questions, she had merely done what she could to stop Sara from going crazy. She had found her a part-time job in the advertising agency Penelope's husband, Roger, ran; and put her up for weeks on end in the spare bedroom until Sara managed to find a one-room flat of her own. The part-time job had become full time, Sara enjoyed the work and was rather better at thinking up copy than she had expected, or, she guessed, than Roger had dared to hope.

Sara had filed for divorce immediately; before she met Peter, whose firm had engaged the agency's services for a short campaign some months after Sara started work. London had been a rather lonely place to her until then; she had hated the crowded streets and her empty room, the smell of diesel fumes, the roar of traffic, the strange, poised threat of the city rising around her. She had felt more isolated and more lonely than she had ever felt in the little cottage by the sea. At least there she had not been afraid to go out at night, afraid to walk home alone, afraid to put out the light when she was in bed.

Peter had changed all that; meeting him had made London less of a wasteland, she had someone in her life who cared about her. In many ways they had similar temperaments. Peter was a typical family man. He would make a marvellous father for the children she wanted so badly, he would be a gentle and considerate husband. He wouldn't dominate her or try to railroad her into giving in to him. He would discuss everything, talk things over, compromise. Alex didn't know the meaning of the word, he had always wanted his own way over everything. Sara would never allow a man to treat her like that again; whenever she thought about Alex she was filled with the anger of having been humiliated, used and manipulated. No man would ever make her despise herself again, that was the promise she had made to herself a year ago, and she meant to keep it.

She hadn't expected to lose her memory. Fate had played a cruel trick on her; flung her back into Alex's power while she was too weak to save herself.

Sara lay on the bed, listening to the sound of the sea outside, the wail of a gull fishing over the waves. Her ears had ceased to beat with angry blood, she was calmer now. She no longer felt dizzy. She cautiously opened her eyes and saw that Alex had left the room, she was alone. She stared at the closed wardrobe, biting her lip. Somehow she had to get away.

Suddenly she heard another vehicle coming down the road. Sliding out of the bed warily, in case her dizziness returned, she crept to the window to look out. At that moment she heard Alex walking down the hall and stiffened. Was he coming back up here?

Her glance shot along the road. The familiar red post office van heading towards the cottage was slowing. They must have mail for Alex. Sara ran back across the room on the tips of her toes, making as little noise as possible. She opened the wardrobe and began to search for something to wear. After she left Alex, her mother had made a visit to the cottage to pack up all Sara's belongings which had later been sent on to London. No wonder Alex had looked distracted as he tried to find her a nightie! Sara looked down at it, frowning. It wasn't hers. Was it Madeleine's?

She shuddered, her mouth distasteful. How could he? She saw a grey track suit hanging in the wardrobe and pulled it down—it would be much too big for her but she could just about get away with running around in it. People didn't take a second look at someone running in a tracksuit, but they would stare like crazy if they saw a woman in a transparent nightie loping about.

She dragged the nightie off and flung it on the floor. She felt like ripping it to pieces but she compromised by kicking it across the room and glaring after it. How dared Alex give her that woman's nightdress to wear? She felt contaminated.

She hurriedly slid into the tracksuit, hoisting up the elasticated waist and belting it tightly just below her breasts with a thin leather belt she found in a drawer. She could hear Alex talking to the postman on the path. They were having an animated conversation about the Derby, which was being run in a day or two.

'Not a chance, Bob,' Alex said loudly. 'Don't chuck your money away. It won't even make the first six.'

'Don't you believe it, Mr Stevenson! I reckon it has a fair old chance.'

'If the other runners break a leg, maybe,' Alex said, laughing.

Sara paused on the landing, hearing their voices below through the open front door. Keep him talking, Mr Postman, she silently pleaded, creeping down the stairs.

'But look at the old form book,' the postman said argumentatively. In this country district there was no hurry, especially when the sun was shining and there was a hazy, summer mist far out over the sea, giving everything a drifting aura of enchantment.

Sara couldn't possibly wear any of Alex's shoes—his feet were sizes bigger. She didn't see why she shouldn't run barefoot in a tracksuit, though. She wasn't likely to meet many people on her way to her parents' home. She heard Alex laughing as she shot down the hall into the kitchen and out of the back door. Sara's teeth met. He sounded pleased with himself—and, of course, he was congratulating himself on his cleverness in caging her upstairs in the bedroom. What had he done with her clothes? Hidden them where she wouldn't find them without a major search?

It wouldn't occur to him that she had escaped until he went upstairs with her lunch, but all the same she was going to have to move fast because the second Alex did discover that she had gone he was going to be coming after her and he moved much faster, his long legs easily outstripping hers.

She went through the long, leafy garden, breathing in the cool scent of lilac and yellow gorse. A rough stone wall enclosed the well-kept garden, she had to clamber over it very carefully, afraid of slipping and banging her head again.

She looked back once at the cottage; the slate roof gleamed in the sunlight above the thick white walls which were built to defy anything the wildest weather could throw at them. It had once been a fisherman's cottage and Sara looked at it with aching regret and nostalgia. After all, she had spent four happy years there; she loved the isolated, embattled little place.

A narrow, sandy path led through a wilderness of bracken, gorse and thorn bushes. Sara stumbled along it, her feet soon sticky with sand and scratched by brambles. She was afraid to run too fast in case her stitches tore loose, but she was afraid to pause for long in case Alex caught up with her. She jogged at a steady pace, ears pricked for sounds of pursuit.

A few minutes later she heard the post office van driving along the road which curved round beside the sea to link up with the new upper road. Sara crouched down among the ferns and peered through them.

She saw the peaked cap of the driver—he was alone. Sara stood up and ran in a zig-zagging movement through the gorse, waving and calling. The driver saw her and slowed, staring.

'Hallo, where did you spring from?' he asked, leaning out of his window. She didn't know him, he was new on this round. Sara sprinted up to the van and leaned on the door, panting.

'Could you give me a lift to the White Abbas turning?' she asked breathlessly, then smiled at him, her eyes coaxing. 'Please?'

He considered her, grinned, tipping back his cap. 'Went for a jog and tired yourself out, did you? Oh, all right, hop in, just this once, although I'm not supposed to, mind!' He had a warm Kent accent and a cheerful smile. He talked as he drove, asking her name and where she lived, said he knew her father, nice chap, and her mother was a lovely lady. He was quite sorry when Sara got out, thanking him.

She was halfway to her parents house when she saw their car coming towards her. Sara halted, waving, and caught sight of her father's stunned expression a second before the car skidded noisily to a stop.

Her mother was out of the car first, running to her. 'Sara! What on earth ... are you all right? What are you doing here? We were just coming over to see you, what are you doing walking about ... and, my God, you haven't got any shoes on! What in heaven's name are you wearing?'

John Calthrop stopped the agitated flow without waiting for Sara to answer any of the questions her mother had flung at her. Putting an arm around his daughter he said quietly, 'Get into the car, Sara, we'll take you home.'

'Not back to the cottage!' she said hoarsely and he looked at her with a stern expression on his thin, tanned face.

'No,' he promised tersely, and Sara collapsed into the back seat of the car, her body limp with relief and exhaustion. Sweat prickled on her skin under the bandage, she felt the wetness of perspiration on her nape under her hair, between her breasts, making the tracksuit cling to her back.

'But what has happened?' her mother demanded as she took the passenger seat next to John Calthrop.

'Molly!' her husband said warningly. 'Leave her alone for the moment, she's tired.'

Molly Calthrop turned to look at him indignantly. 'I can see that, but she shouldn't be wandering around in her state. Can't I even ask . . .'

'Later,' John Calthrop said, and his wife sank back in her seat with an impatient sigh.

A few moments later they pulled up outside the Calthrop home and Sara shakily got out of the car. Her mother unlocked the front door while her father put an arm around Sara, watching her anxiously.

'You look ill,' he said.

'I feel rotten.' Sara leant her head on his wiry shoulder, feeling like crying but refusing to give in to that weakness. Her parents had been coming to see her, they hadn't swallowed whatever Alex had told them, they were worried and it made her feel slightly better to know that she could, at least, depend on them to take her side against her ex-husband. When she had suspected that her father was inclined to take Alex's side she had been very hurt. She had always been closer to her father than her mother, she needed John Calthrop's sympathy and understanding.

'I think we ought to call a doctor,' her father thought aloud.

'The hospital told me to come back if I had any problems. I think I should go there. I think I've got concussion.' What else explained it? The X-rays hadn't revealed any skull damage but her amnesia, the dizziness, the weakness she felt had to have some explanation. Sara was scared. What if there was something seriously wrong with her?

Her father steered her into the house but before she had summoned the strength to climb the stairs they all heard the throb of a car engine and the whine of tyres travelling fast on a hot road. The car skidded to a stop outside and Sara began to shake.

'It's Alex,' she said, looking pleadingly at her father.

'Yes, I know.' John Calthrop was frowning angrily. 'Sara, go upstairs. I'll deal with Alex.'

GIVE YOUR HEART TO HARLEQUIN®

FREE!

Mail this heart today!

AND WE'LL GIVE YOU 4 FREE BOOKS, A FREE PEN AND WATCH SET, AND A FREE MYSTERY GIFT!

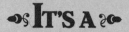 ❧ IT'S A ❧

HARLEQUIN HONEYMOON
A SWEETHEART
OF A FREE OFFER!

4 NEW "HARLEQUIN PRESENTS"—FREE! Take a "Harlequin Honeymoon" with four exciting romances—yours FREE from Harlequin Reader Service! Each of these hot-off-the-presses novels brings you all the passion and tenderness of today's greatest love stories…your free passports to bright new worlds of love and foreign adventure!

But wait…there's <u>even more</u> to this great <u>free offer</u>…

HARLEQUIN PEN AND WATCH SET—ABSOLUTELY FREE! You'll love your personal Harlequin Pen and Watch Set. Perfect for daytime…elegant enough for evening. The watch has a genuine leather strap and replaceable battery. The watch and the stylish matching pen are yours free with this offer!

SPECIAL EXTRAS—FREE! You'll get our free monthly newsletter, packed with news on your favorite writers, upcoming books, and more. Four times a year, you'll receive our members' magazine, Harlequin Romance Digest!

<u>Best of all,</u> you'll periodically <u>receive our special-edition "Harlequin Bestsellers," yours to preview for ten days without charge!</u>

MONEY-SAVING HOME DELIVERY! Join Harlequin Reader Service and enjoy the <u>convenience</u> of previewing eight new books every month, delivered right to your home. Each book is yours for only $1.75—<u>20¢ less per book</u> than what you pay in stores! Great savings plus total convenience add up to a sweetheart of a deal for <u>you</u>!

PU 8/85

START YOUR HARLEQUIN HONEYMOON TODAY—
JUST COMPLETE, DETACH & MAIL YOUR FREE OFFER CARD!

HARLEQUIN READER SERVICE
❧ FREE OFFER CARD ❧

**PLACE HEART
STICKER HERE**

FREE
PEN AND
WATCH SET

FREE
HOME
DELIVERY

PLUS AN
EXTRA BONUS
"MYSTERY
GIFT"!

4 FREE
BOOKS

☐ YES! Please send me my four HARLEQUIN PRESENTS® books, free, along with my free Pen and Watch Set and Mystery Gift! Then send me eight new HARLEQUIN PRESENTS books every month, as they come off the presses, and bill me at just $1.75 per book (20¢ less than retail), with no extra charges for shipping and handling. If I am not completely satisfied, I may return a shipment and cancel at any time. The free books, Pen, Watch and Mystery Gift remain mine to keep!

108 CIP CAJ8

FIRST NAME_____LAST NAME_____
(PLEASE PRINT)

ADDRESS_____APT._____

CITY_____

PROV./STATE_____POSTAL CODE/ZIP_____

PRINTED IN U.S.A.

BUSINESS REPLY CARD

First Class   Permit No. 717   Buffalo, NY

Postage will be paid by addressee

Harlequin® Reader Service

901 Fuhrmann Blvd.,

P.O. Box 1394

Buffalo, NY 14240-9963

NO POSTAGE
NECESSARY
IF MAILED
IN THE
UNITED STATES

CHAPTER SIX

SARA didn't wait to discuss the matter, she almost ran up the stairs with her mother on her heels saying: 'Sara! Be careful!' Behind them Sara heard the thud of Alex's feet as he ran up the path and she was so terrified that he would talk his way past her father that she ignored her mother's anxiety and hurtled into the room she always used when she was at home. Her mother followed, protesting, and Sara slammed the door and bolted it.

'What are you doing?' Molly Calthrop asked, staring.

Sara sat down abruptly on the bed. She felt her ears buzzing again, she was afraid that ghastly vertigo was about to begin. She kept very still, trying to relax. Downstairs she heard the deep angry tones of Alex's voice and the answering anger of her father.

'Why is Alex shouting?' Molly Calthrop asked, moving back to the door.

'Don't open it!' Sara yelled, tensing.

'Sara! What is going on?' Her mother came back and sat down beside her, put an arm round her shoulders. 'I wish someone would tell me what is happening.' She sounded plaintive now and Sara sighed, forcing a wry smile.

'Oh, Mum!' She looked into the face which was so much like her own; at closer quarters you

could see Molly Calthrop's real age although
from a distance she could have been anything
from thirty to forty-five. The delicacy of her
features and slender body gave no hint of that
down-to-earth nature. She looked as if a summer
breeze could lift her off her feet, yet she was
practical and untroubled by the doubts and
uncertainties that put the haunted look into
Sara's green eyes at times. Sara wished suddenly
that she had inherited her mother's temperament
as well as her physical build. It must make life so
much easier.

'Why won't anyone tell me? Molly Calthrop
complained. 'Your father said you had had a
slight accident on your way back to London but
it was nothing to worry about, you would be okay
in a day or two. He said you were staying at the
cottage with Alex and I thought . . .' Her mother
broke off, shrugging. 'Well, never mind that—
what were you doing walking along the road just
now in those peculiar clothes?'

Sara looked down at them, grimacing. 'I look a
sight, don't I?'

'You look like a clown,' her mother said
frankly, laughing.

Sara got up and began to take them off. A pink
towelling robe hung on the back of the door, as it
always did, in case a visiting member of the
family needed to borrow it. Sara slid into it,
naked, and tied the belt firmly.

Her mother studied her. 'Well, at least you
look less ridiculous,' she conceded. She patted
the bed beside her. 'Sit down and tell me what is
happening.'

Sara sat down. 'It's complicated,' she sighed and began to explain about her amnesia. Her mother became very agitated as she went on and occasionally broke out with incoherent comments.

'Alex had no right . . .'

Sara shrugged at that; when had Alex ever bothered to consider what right he had to do anything?

'It could be very serious, we must get you to a hospital at once . . .'

'I think so,' Sara agreed.

'Head injuries are so worrying!'

Sara's attention was divided between her mother and the argument still raging downstairs. She couldn't make out which of the two men was winning; they both sounded obstinate.

'I'm amazed that Alex took such a risk with you!'

Alex was always taking risks with everything; he didn't see what he did as a risk, he was too self-assured, too certain he was right and couldn't lose.

'He should have taken you straight back to the hospital!'

'Oh, he didn't want to do that,' Sara said cynically. That hadn't been his plan, at all; her amnesia had been far too convenient for him, an absolute godsend, an unexpected windfall.

'You shouldn't have hidden it from the doctor, either, come to that,' her mother said, thinking hard.

'I thought I'd simply forgotten the few days before the accident, I'd no idea how bad it was—

but Alex knew.' He knew and he took advantage of it ruthlessly. At least her parents could now see him in his true light, she wouldn't have them constantly urging her to forgive him and start again.

'Alex should have told you!' Mollie Calthrop protested, far too straightforward herself to recognise the twists and turns of a more devious nature.

Sara smiled drily. 'Oh, yes, he should have—but he didn't. Didn't I tell you he was unscrupulous?'

Her mother looked at her, eyes wide, lips parted on a gasp. 'I've always been so fond of him,' she said wistfully. 'Poor Alex.'

'Oh, Mother!' Sara groaned. 'Don't call him that—how can you after what he's done to me?'

'I can only think that he didn't understand how serious it might be, and hoped it would give him a chance to straighten out the problems between you,' her mother thought aloud. With incredulity Sara realised that Molly Calthrop was already looking for a way of forgiving Alex, finding excuses for him. It wasn't the first time she had realised that people will go to any lengths to excuse the behaviour of someone they care for, whereas identical behaviour from someone they dislike is furiously attacked. People weren't consistent or rational all the time; they thought with their hearts as much as their heads.

'He loves you very much,' Molly Calthrop said coaxingly and Sara looked at her with weary disbelief.

'He has a weird way of showing it!'

'Alex doesn't find it easy to admit his feelings,' her mother quickly defended. 'Don't you know that? You ought to, Sara, he's your husband, you should know him better than you seem to—he had such a lonely childhood, nobody to love or to love him, he didn't learn how to show his feelings the way most children do, from their parents. He learnt to lock his emotions inside himself, hide them, keep a guard on his tongue, never give anything away.'

'Is this what he's been telling you?' Sara felt a peculiar stab of pain because Alex had talked to her mother in a way he had never talked to her. Through all the years of their marriage Alex had stayed separate, made taboo any form of confidence which might reveal him to her. He had always been so strong and self-sufficient; he hadn't needed Sara. He had owned her, but she had never possessed Alex.

'Not in so many words, he's far too proud, but I can read between the lines, even if you can't.'

Sara laughed bitterly. 'Maybe you read more than was there!'

A tap on the door made them both jump. Molly gave her daughter an uncertain glance, lifting her brows.

'Shall I open it?'

'Who is it?' Sara called, holding her voice steady with an effort.

'Me,' her father said quietly. 'Alex has gone—open this door, Sara.'

Molly Calthrop got up and walked across the room while Sara sagged, closing her eyes on a deep sigh of relief, weakness and resented pain.

Alex had gone. She ought to be glad—she *was* glad, she insisted. The only reason why she felt she might burst into tears was that she was ill.

Her father came in and looked questioningly at her. 'How do you feel now?'

'I'm going to be okay,' she said doggedly. When she had recovered from this head wound she would be deeply relieved to have got out of the trap Alex had set for her. She had escaped by the skin of her teeth. She felt sick at the very thought of what might have happened—undoubtedly would have happened—if Madeleine hadn't chosen to put in an appearance and prompted her memory. Alex had so nearly managed to seduce her. He had intended to, sooner or later; he had only held back because he was handling her carefully while she was in shock. It wouldn't have been long before he had had her—and if he had, she would be hating herself even more than she did now. How could she help feeling bitter self-contempt every time she remembered those moments in the bed, in his arms, her mind dissolving in the heated exchange of a desire she had been so pathetically certain she had killed long ago. It hadn't died—it had only been sleeping, and Alex had had no trouble reawakening it.

John Calthrop was studying her soberly, his hazel eyes sharp with anxiety. 'All the same, I'm taking you back to the hospital. It's time you told them about your amnesia; that may be a side effect they'll take very seriously.'

Sara didn't argue, she was too worried. There was something so disturbing about having lost whole chunks of your life even if only for twenty-four hours.

Looking at the pink robe she was wearing she said wryly: 'What am I going to wear? I suppose Alex didn't bring my clothes back? He's got my suitcase at the cottage.'

Her father scratched his ear, looking baffled. 'He didn't mention it.'

'You can borrow some of my clothes,' Mollie Calthrop said. 'Come and choose something now—the sooner we get you to the hospital the better I shall feel.'

Sara giggled as she looked at the pretty floral cotton dresses her mother liked to wear. 'I don't see myself in these!'

Her mother looked indulgent. 'No, they're not your style, are they? How about my denim suit, though?'

Sara's face brightened as her mother took the olive green pants suit out of the wardrobe. Sara had nudged her mother into buying it and Molly had rarely worn it; it wasn't her style any more than the flowered cotton was Sara's. Stylishly cut on simple lines it was in the very latest fashion.

'Now you're talking,' Sara said, draping it over her arm. 'Have you got a shirt to go with it?'

She went back into her bedroom and changed quickly. Her parents were downstairs waiting for her, she heard them talking as she went down to join them. They sounded upset and on edge but the minute they heard Sara coming they stopped talking and looked round with bright, unreal smiles.

'You look very good in that,' her father said, 'why don't you ever wear it, Molly? I like it.'

'Not on me, you don't,' she said tartly. 'The only time I put it on you said "What on earth is that?" and I put it back into the wardrobe.'

He made a wry face. 'Well, it suits Sara.' He put an arm around his daughter and guided her out of the house protectively while Mollie followed in the rear. Sara got into the back seat and her father closed the car door, walking round to get into the driver's seat while his wife was locking the front door of the house. At that second the telephone began to ring and Sara stiffened.

'Don't answer it, it's Alex,' she said urgently.

Her father frowned. 'It may not be—he only left here a few minutes ago.'

'I'll see who it is,' Molly Calthrop said, hurrying back into the house. Sara stared out of the car window, watching the late afternoon shadows eating up the trees and flowers. Birds flitted from branch to branch, one of her mother's cats prowled below the trees, his eye cocked hopefully, and the sweet, heavy scent of night flowering stock and dark red musky wallflowers made the air cloyingly nostalgic.

Her mother came out of the house and got into the car. She looked round calmly. 'It was Peter, ringing from abroad somewhere.'

Sara sat upright. 'Why didn't you call me to speak to him?'

'He was in a hurry. I told him about your accident and that we were taking you back to the hospital now to have a check-up because you'd had a touch of concussion and he was very worried and said I wasn't to bother you, he'd ring again this evening to find out how you were.' Molly Calthrop made it all sound so reasonable but her explanation seemed lame to Sara. Her mother didn't like Peter as much as she liked Alex; she gave him no encouragement, that was why she hadn't bothered to call Sara to the phone. She hadn't wanted her to talk to Peter.

'Well, when he rings back, I want to talk to him,' Sara said in a faintly sulky voice. She wanted to accuse her mother of interfering, but she knew Molly would deny it, perhaps wasn't even conscious of her own instinctive reaction. Molly was a conservative woman who hated changes in her private world; she had become fond of Alex and didn't want him to disappear from the family circle.

From the moment that she left Alex, Sara had been aware of an unremitting pressure from her whole family, urging her to forgive him and try again. Seen from the outside, no doubt it might seem possible, even a wise thing to do. From all that her family had seen of that marriage, it had been a great success. Sara had been happy for four years, Alex had made himself one of them, they were proud of having a famous son-in-law or brother-in-law. The surface of Sara's marriage had been so smooth and glossy, no one else had had a chance to see the infinitesimal cracks below the patina or to recognise the possibility that one day they might widen beyond repair and the whole thing shatter.

When she first broke the news to them she had

been showered with advice and comfort. Her parents, her sister, her brothers, had all told her that nothing and nobody was perfect, everyone had flaws, people made mistakes, these things happen, if a marriage has been happy it can be put together again, all that was needed was a little tolerance and understanding. She had been fierce with resentment, bitter with humiliation, their advice had been a whole string of truisms and clichés that she saw as meaningless, the only result of their well-meaning intervention had been that Sara had fled to London to get away from it, and them.

She knew that they saw Alex's affair with his secretary as one little slip—never to be repeated, much regretted. Alex had talked to them, too, separately, since Sara would not see him. He had given them his side of the story and part of Sara's resentment had been because she knew that Alex had been given more sympathy than she had. He was the straying lamb, who should be taken back into the fold. She was the hard, unforgiving wife who refused to have the humanity to save him from a secretary on the make. They hated Madeleine even more than Sara did—she got all the blame in the affair, but then they were not married to Alex, they weren't left with a bitter taste in their mouths because Alex had betrayed them. They weren't jealous . . .

Sara jerked away from admitting that, frowning, as they drove away from the coast inland towards Ashford through the green and gold of a summer afternoon.

She saw the same doctor she had seen before and he looked at her probingly as he recognised her in turn.

'Back again? Problems?'

She told him about the amnesia and he leaned back in his chair, tapping a silver pencil on his desk, frowning.

'Why didn't you tell me this at the time?' he asked, not unreasonably.

'I didn't realise . . .' It sounded lame and she knew it, flushing as he turned a wry stare on her. His face silently told her she was an idiot but that he wasn't too surprised by that, most of his patients were halfwits who omitted vital facts from their recitals of symptoms and worries.

'But now you've remembered everything?' he questioned and she nodded, but told him about the attack of vertigo which she had had immediately after she recovered her memory.

He nodded, asked a few more questions about the dizziness. Had she been sick? Had she had headaches or any problems with vision? How long since the vertigo? How soon had it passed? No return of the giddy feeling?

'Your X-rays were fine, no sign of any fracture,' he said thoughtfully. 'But maybe we should have you in a bed here for a day or two just to keep an eye on you in case the concussion is more serious than we'd thought.'

'Is that sort of amnesia common?' Sara asked and he told her that it wasn't unusual.

'It may well be connected more with the shock of the crash than your actual head injury,' he added. 'Shock is unpredictable, it has some strange side effects. We'll keep you in for a short time and run a few more tests.'

She had a few words with her parents before a nurse took her off to a sunlit ward on the upper floor of the hospital. 'When Peter rings, tell him not to worry, the doctor didn't seem too concerned about the amnesia. I'm only being kept here as a precaution and I should be out within a few days. There's no need for Peter to panic into flying home. I'll see him in London when he gets back.'

Mrs Calthrop shrugged Peter aside. 'Is there anything we can get you?' she asked. 'We'll come over to see you tomorrow, visiting hours are at six.'

'I'd like something to read and my tiny transistor with the headphones, please. If you can persuade Alex to hand over my case, you'll find them in there.'

'I'll ring Alex as soon as we get home,' her mother promised with far more readiness and warmth than she had shown when Sara gave her the message for Peter. 'He'll be very worried,' she added and Sara eyed her crossly.

'You're so transparent, Mother!'

'And you're very unkind,' Molly Calthrop burst out. 'Do you think Alex is without human feelings? When he first heard about your accident he rang us before he drove to get you and he was very upset, I could tell.'

'Oh, you could tell, could you?' Sara snapped. 'You're cleverer than I am, then, because I can never guess anything about his real reactions. He's a damned sight more deceptive than you realise.'

Her mother flushed, bridling, but then the nurse tapped on the waiting-room door and after quickly kissing her parents Sara followed her out of the room.

Over the next two days she had a series of tests and saw several specialists. The hospital kept her under close observation but there was no recurrence of the vertigo, nor did she have any headaches or problems with her vision. Apart from the cut on her head, she seemed to be perfectly normal, and on the second day she largely lay in bed reading and listening to music on her headphones. She slept a good deal, too; she was very tired. Emotion had that effect on her, it burned up all her energy.

On the Thursday morning her father collected her and drove her back to the marsh to the Calthrop home. The weather was faintly misty but a pale sun was trying to break through, shining behind the opalescent mist like a ragged orange flower behind a veil. Sara had had her bandages changed before she left; the nurse had renewed them with a square of elasticated bandage strapped neatly with one thin piece of gauze to secure it.

'You look quite romantic in that,' her father teased. 'An interesting invalid.'

She laughed. 'I thought I looked like a pirate, myself. All I need is a parrot on my shoulder.' She watched the mist lifting over the shimmering sea; from somewhere deep within the mist came the hoarse moan of a foghorn.

'I rang your office, by the way,' John Calthrop told her.

'Oh, good. I forgot all about them until yesterday. I suppose they wondered what on earth had happened to me?'

'Your boss said he guessed something was wrong when there was no reply from your flat, he had been intending to ring me but I got to him first.'

'Did you tell him that the doctor thinks I should have several weeks off? I have to go back to have the stitches out next Wednesday, they'll tell me then when I can go back to work.'

'You'd better stay on with us until they're sure you are really well,' her father said and Sara shifted to look at him, her eyes defiant.

'I'm fine, I can look after myself.' He eyed her with a wry smile while she was speaking, shaking his head.

'Don't be silly, Sara. What's the point of going back to that tiny flat? I don't think you should be alone until the doctor is quite certain the dizziness won't start again—if you fell you could hurt yourself badly, and nobody would be there to help you.' He patted her hand. 'It's all very well being independent but there's such a thing as taking it too far.'

She bit her lip, frowning, not wishing to tell him her real reason for wanting to get back to London. She was terrified of being within such a short distance of the cottage; Alex could walk across any time and catch her before she could get away. Her father was out most days from half-past eight to six or even seven. Her mother had to go shopping and visiting friends. Sara would inevitably be left alone occasionally—what if Alex picked that time to call at the house?

Her parents wouldn't conspire with him, though, would they? They knew she was dead set against seeing him and that she would be angry if they warned Alex when she would be alone. Nevertheless, Sara didn't feel easy about staying on in the marsh. Alex had powerful telescopes and binoculars which he used to watch vessels passing along the coast. This was the busiest sea passage in the world; a continual procession of ships passed through the English Channel, there was always something interesting to see and Alex was a yachtsman who was fascinated by the sea and ships. He loved sea birds, too, and often watched them through binoculars, studying their feeding and mating habits while he lay among the sandy dunes on the beach.

Even if her parents didn't tip him off whenever she was alone in the house, Alex might still be able to keep a check on all their movements with those powerful binoculars of his—but would he go to such lengths? Sara grimaced. Was she getting paranoid? It wouldn't be surprising if she was—Alex would make anyone paranoid. If he decided he would see her, whatever her wishes, he would find a way and that probably meant that she wouldn't even be safe from him in London.

He had left her strictly alone for over a year, but during that time he hadn't had any encouragement to believe she might ever forgive him. While she didn't remember Madeleine Bentley she had given him all the encouragement he had needed, and Alex's attitude had changed.

Sara was as sure of that as she was certain that she was more under threat now than she had been

since the day she first walked out on him. Alex
had no scruples about pursuing an advantage—
the question was, what would he do now? And to
that Sara had no answer. She wished she knew.

Her mother opened the front door to them a
few minutes later and one look at her face made
the hair bristle on the back of Sara's neck. She
halted in mid-step backing like a panic-stricken
mule, head back and eyes wary.

'There's someone waiting to see you!' her
mother said, her manner one of suppressed
excitement.

'I won't see him!' Sara burst out hoarsely.

Mrs Calthrop stared back at her, apparently
amazed, although why she should pretend to be
so surprised when Sara had made it crystal clear
how she felt about Alex left Sara baffled. How
many times did she have to spell it out? When
would they start believing that she knew what she
wanted and what she meant?

'Hang on, Sara! Don't get so upset, you don't
even know who it is yet,' her father said in the
firm, yet gentle, voice she remembered so well
from her childhood. She looked at him in
agitation, her face flushed.

'Of course I do! And you can just tell Alex
that . . .'

'It isn't Alex!' Mrs Calthrop interrupted and
Sara looked incredulously at her. She had been so
sure that it was—maybe she *was* becoming
paranoid? But if it wasn't Alex, who else could
put that excitement into her mother's eyes?
Certainly not Peter, her mother wouldn't look
like that for him. Disapproval and reproach

would stare out of her face, not a glowing excitement.

'Then who . . .?'

'Mr Jonas,' Mrs Calthrop said happily, smiling. 'Isn't it kind of him to call to see you? Alex had told him about your accident and he was worried about you, so while he was down in this part of the world he thought he would stop by and see how you were.'

Sara was staring fixedly at her, hearing what she said in another voice, not her mother's, the deceptively laid-back, drawling tones of Leonard Jonas, the head of Empire Films, the only man who could make Alex come running when he clicked his fingers. LJ was what Alex might well be in another twenty years—he was the blueprint on which Alex had cut himself. Ruthless, opportunist, cool-headed and shrewd, the man had always made Sara nervous and once she had left Alex she had hoped never to see LJ again.

What was he doing here?

CHAPTER SEVEN

'Do you feel well enough to be able to talk to him?' her father asked, his brow corrugated, and she hesitated, because he was giving her the chance to get out of seeing LJ, and maybe that was what she ought to do. What could Alex's boss have to say to her that she wanted to hear? His motive for coming to see her had to be connected with Alex and the last thing she needed was pressure from yet another quarter on the subject of Alex.

'He's driven over just to see you!' her mother protested. Molly Calthrop was impressed by LJ, that was obvious, and Sara wasn't surprised by it. Her mother liked men like that—it had been on the cards that she would be bowled over by Leonard Jonas just as it had been on the cards that Alex would soon become a favourite with her. Sara looked at her mother wryly, understanding her. Her mother was ultra-feminine; she was drawn to ultra-macho men, especially those who had drive and were very successful.

'I suppose I'd better see him,' Sara admitted reluctantly. She was curious to know why LJ was here, anyway. She was sure she could guess—but she might as well find out for certain.

Molly Calthrop beamed on her. 'Of course you must. Go in and talk to him and I'll bring some coffee and biscuits.'

'Sure you're not too tired?' John Calthrop asked and Sara patted his arm.

'I'm fine, Dad.' She was grateful for his concern, it made her feel protected. Her father's eyes had a look of shy tenderness which they often wore when he looked at her. He couldn't express his love for her as openly and easily as he had when she was a child—any more than she could show him how much she loved him. When did the inhibitions begin? she wondered. During early teens when she was suddenly rebellious and touchy and wouldn't be kissed or hugged? She had grown out of that but things had never been the same again. Small children can happily climb on to a parent's lap and cuddle close—gawky adolescents can never bring themselves to be so demonstrative, however much they may need love. Their gestures of love become the secretive delight between lovers, caresses given and received in private in a very different temperature. Passion has a fiercer colour than affection; for a time it burns out the paler shades of family fondness.

Sara smiled at her father and went into the sitting-room. Leonard Jonas was standing with his back to her, studying the photographs on the long, oak sideboard. She watched him turn as he heard the door open and close.

'Sara! Wonderful to see you—it's been too long.' He rambled over; a tall, stooped, rangy man in late middle-age, with leathery skin and light grey eyes. Sara offered her cheek and he bent to kiss it.

'Hallo, LJ.' She looked at his fleshless face,

wondering exactly how old he really was—he was so spare and full of energy that it was hard to tell. He lived on a peculiar diet of nuts, fruit and salad. Alex said LJ meant to live for ever and during the five years Sara had known him, LJ had hardly altered an inch, he never seemed to age.

'Sorry to hear about your accident, my dear. Sit down, sit down, you shouldn't be standing around. We must take care of you, head injuries are no fun.'

Sara sat down in an armchair and LJ folded himself up on the couch facing her, his hands on his knees. He always dressed casually, even in London; today he wore a grey and red check shirt with light grey pants belted at the waist. A casual observer, noticing him, would never have guessed that he was a man of great power and influence with a personal fortune which could only be vaguely estimated. You had to watch LJ in operation to realise that he was a man to be treated with respect and caution.

'You just got out of hospital today?' he asked and she nodded. 'Everything okay?' LJ added and she smiled, nodding again. 'Glad to hear it,' he said. 'We're too fond of you to lose you,' he murmured, making a familiar gesture to underline the remark. LJ had a habit of emphasising what he said with stabs of one crooked, index finger. He was a very emphatic man. In many ways Alex was very like him. Sara could never decide whether Alex had deliberately modelled himself on the older man or whether it was entirely natural. They both had vitality and force of personality, but LJ was an innate politician. He manipulated people shrewdly and had an intuitive understanding of what made human beings tick.

'It's kind of you to visit me,' Sara said with faint dryness because she was wondering why he had come, and how soon he would get to the real reason for his visit.

'Not at all, I haven't seen you for months and I was very concerned when Alex told me about your accident.'

Mrs Calthrop came into the room with a tray of coffee and biscuits which LJ accepted with smiling alacrity. 'I'm a great coffee drinker, Mrs Calthrop—a real addict, I run on the stuff. No, no cream, thank you, I take it black without sugar.'

'The same for me!' Sara said as her mother picked up the cream jug and Mrs Calthrop gave her a reproachful look.

'You know black coffee isn't good for you, especially now.'

'It won't hurt me,' Sara said, bridling at her mother's scolding tone. Did she think Sara was still twelve? Mrs Calthrop handed her the cup, her mouth compressed. Her face changed, though, when she looked at LJ.

'Will you stay for lunch, Mr Jonas?'

'I'd have loved that,' he said at once, his face regretful. 'But I'm in a tearing hurry to get back to town, I'm afraid. I hope you'll ask me again some other time?' Sara watched ruefully as her mother glowed, backing out of the room. LJ might be coming close to sixty but he still had an

undeniable sex appeal—or perhaps power was an
aphrodisiac which did not diminish with age?

'You've made a conquest,' she teased. 'My
mother thinks you're wonderful.'

LJ grinned at her, briefly almost boyish. 'She's
a very attractive woman—you're very like her,
aren't you? I spotted the resemblance the minute
she opened the door. Ah ha! I thought, so that's
how the chicken got out of the egg?'

Sara laughed and took a sip of coffee which
almost went down the wrong way, choking her, as
LJ suddenly asked: 'Are you still in love with
Alex?'

Sara coughed, her hand shaking as she put
down the coffee. She made rather more of a
performance out of clearing her throat than was
necessary; it gave her time to think. Time to get
angry, too. How dared he come down here and
ask her such brutal, personal questions? She
hardly knew him, what right did he think he had?

LJ put down his cup, too, and rose, looking
worried. 'Are you okay, Sara?' He fussed over
her, patting her on the shoulders.

'I'm all right,' she muttered when she could
speak again and LJ slowly sat down again. 'Did
Alex send you here?' Sara asked coolly, staring at
him without a smile.

'No, no,' he said too quickly. 'He doesn't even
know I'm here—he thinks I'm driving back to
London after spending a night at the cottage to
talk business with him.' He stabbed the air with
that crooked finger, leaning towards her. 'A year
ago, when you walked out on Alex, he asked me
not to interfere but I'm going to have to . . .'

'Why?' Sara interrupted fiercely. 'I'm sorry, but it's no business of yours, Mr Jonas.'

'It certainly is,' he said flatly. 'Alex is like a son to me. I've never had a child of my own, you know. My wife couldn't have children.' He gave a shrug. 'It was just one of those things, she offered to divorce me so I could marry again and have some kids but I didn't want any other woman. If it was Leah and no kids, or kids and no Leah, I knew which I preferred.'

Sara sat back, silenced by the calm simplicity of the statement. She had often wondered why LJ had no children, his happy marriage was a byword in a business not famous for successful matrimony.

'That's beside the point, though,' LJ steamrollered on. 'It's Alex that concerns me at the moment. On Monday I sent my secretary down to the cottage with a script for Alex . . .'

'Your secretary?' Sara broke in with a breathless surprise. Did he mean that Madeleine had taken his secretary's place and brought the script down herself? Or that . . .

'Madeleine Bentley,' LJ supplied, studying her wryly. 'Didn't you know she had moved into my office? Oh, yes, Alex asked me to take her off his hands a year ago. He couldn't stand having her around him any more, but she's a first-class assistant and he thought she'd be useful to me.' His eyes held cynicism and amusement. 'I'm too old and too cute a bird to be snared by her sort of female and anyway I've never fancied anyone but Leah. Madeleine was no problem to me.'

'But she was a problem to Alex?' Sara said,

frowning and trying to work out Alex's motivation. Why had he had Madeleine transferred to LJ's office? Was their affair over? Was Alex afraid she would make him marry her when his divorce was through? All this explained the odd atmosphere she had sensed between Alex and Madeleine as they talked on the path outside the cottage the other day. They hadn't sounded like lovers, there had been an edgy feel to their voices.

'She's a tough cookie,' LJ said, sounding wry and admiring. 'I'll probably be promoting her very soon, she has a future in front of her, that girl. Mind like a razor blade.' He shifted, picking up his cup and drinking some coffee. 'Where was I? Oh, yes, when she came down with the script she saw you in the bedroom and she told me about it when she got back. Naturally, I jumped to the conclusion that you and Alex were together again and I was very relieved.'

Sara eyed him sardonically. 'Were you?' He still hadn't convinced her that her marriage had anything to do with him, but short of walking out of this room she knew there was no way of shutting him up. LJ was accustomed to giving his unadulterated views and having them listened to with respect. He meant to give her his opinion about her marriage and he wasn't going to let her stop him.

He prodded the air with that finger again, nodding. The neck protruding from his shirt collar was thin and bony, it was the most obvious clue to his age.

'Honey, since you left, Alex hasn't been the same man. I've been pretty worried about him.

His temper has been unpredictable, he's been moody and difficult, his work has been patchy. A guy like Alex needs a stabiliser, he runs on his nerves, you know that. When he's high, he's out of sight and nobody can catch him, but when he hits a low, it can mean disaster for everyone. I need Alex riding high, he's a brilliant director with an inventive mind, he has style, not too many of our directors can give me that.'

'I'm sorry,' Sara said coldly. 'Alex's moods have nothing to do with me.'

'They have everything to do with you. While he had you, his work was better than ever before. Since you went, he can't concentrate and it has been months since he really worked. I've sent him barrels of scripts, he turns them all down. The light has gone out inside him. I want it lit again, and damn soon.'

Sara got up stiffly. 'I'm not on your payroll, Mr Jonas. You can't arrange my life to suit your company. My marriage is over and I'm divorcing Alex. If that interferes with your plans, I'm sorry, but I only have one life to live and I'm living it for myself, not for you.'

He waved an irritated hand at her. 'Sit down, sit down, I haven't finished.'

'I have,' Sara said in an impeded voice, wanting to scream at him but forced to pretend courtesy.

He bent forward, the veins in his thin neck like knotted cords, almost navy blue under his skin. 'Alex loves you, damn you!'

'If he had, he wouldn't have had an affair with Madeleine Bentley!'

LJ wiped a hand over his face as though to erase the marks of his irritation. 'Sit down, will you! How can I talk to you while you keep trying to walk out?'

Sara sat, but only because she was afraid he might have a stroke out of pure temper if she disobeyed him. LJ wasn't accustomed to being contradicted or thwarted.

'Look, I'm going to straighten out this whole tangle and get Alex back to work,' LJ said impatiently. 'There was no affair with Madeleine.'

'Oh, really . . .' Sara muttered, too furious to let him get away with that. 'Don't tell me fairy tales, Mr Jonas! I had all that from Alex and I didn't believe a word of it.'

The beetling brows met over LJ's long, arrogant nose. 'You didn't believe him?' he repeated and there was scathing contempt in his stare. 'Alex gave me his word on it, woman, and his word is good enough for me!'

'If they didn't have an affair, why would Madeleine say they did? Why did her husband have all that evidence? What about the hotel staff who saw them in bedrooms at night? What about the love letter? The photographs?' Sara's voice had risen and she was shaking with pain and anger. Did he think she enjoyed discussing all that? When was she going to be able to forget it all? These embers kept on smouldering and, as she had bitterly discovered, it took the slightest breeze to fan them into flame again.

'Lies,' LJ said angrily.

Sara laughed, her eyes incredulous. 'You really

expect me to believe that? I talked to her husband, the man was very upset.'

'Oh, he believed them,' LJ said, his mouth twisting distastefully. 'The liar is Madeleine.'

Sara sat back in stunned silence and LJ leaned forward to catch hold of her hands and squeeze them firmly. He liked personal contact, it helped to get over what he was trying to say, he was always patting a shoulder or hugging someone.

'Listen to me, Sara, I know what I'm talking about—Madeleine pursued him and Alex wasn't quick enough to spot what she was after, that's all. Sure, her husband had evidence that they had connecting rooms when they were abroad, and sure, Madeleine would come through into Alex's room to have a drink with him after a long day. She was his secretary, when he'd finished filming he dictated notes and letters to her, memos to me, ideas for the next day's work. He couldn't work with her in a bar, for God's sake. It had to be in his room; it wasn't just a bedroom, it was a suite. Alex worked late, he always does. Sometimes it would be midnight before he went upstairs, but that doesn't mean anything.'

'And the love letter?' Sara asked drily.

LJ looked into her eyes, grimacing. 'I told you—Madeleine was after Alex. She didn't get him, honey. When he realised what was in her mind, he asked me to take her off his hands. If she hadn't been so good at her job he'd just have fired her, but he knew I'd be glad to have her. I'd already noticed her and talked to him about her. She's a lady that means to get noticed, she made sure I didn't pass her over.'

She clutched his wiry, dry-skinned hands, staring at him. He clearly believed he was telling the truth—but had Alex lied to him? If he hadn't, if Alex had always been innocent, why had he refused to tell her what LJ had just told her? Why had he merely insisted that she accept his unsupported word?

LJ rubbed his thumbs over the back of her hands, the rhythmic little caress soothing, watching her intently to see the effect of his words.

'Doesn't it seem odd to you that Alex could confide in you, but refuse to explain any of this to me?' she asked harshly.

LJ considered her, his eyes thoughtful. 'Alex is a complicated fella, my dear. Perhaps he wanted you to make some special gesture—he wanted proof that you loved him enough to trust him, or trusted him enough to go on loving him. Who knows?'

'Wasn't that asking a lot?' Sara said in a shaking voice, her face white.

'If you say so,' LJ murmured and she felt that he was judging her, finding her a disappointment. It was unfair but Sara wouldn't argue with him, she pulled her hands free and stood up.

'Well, it was kind of you to want to help,' she said politely and LJ stood up, too, his expression impatient.

'Sara, you have a happy home here, I can see how nice your parents are and what a good childhood you must have had—haven't you ever considered what Alex's childhood did to him? It's always there, at the back of his mind. You can't shake off the first fifteen years of your life, you know. They form you. Whatever you are as an adult you became as a child. He had nobody and he didn't know who he was—he was a born outsider and he must have wanted badly to get inside and have a home and family of his own.'

Sara walked to the door, her face in shadow as she turned away. LJ thought he knew Alex so well, but there were hidden tracts of Alex's nature that LJ had never seen. Alex hadn't wanted a family, he had refused to have children. His idea of family life was to have a woman quietly tucked away, not bothering him when he was busy, a woman to fall back on when his glamorous life palled a little but who he could walk away from with impunity when he tired of her company. Sara wasn't going to talk about that to LJ. No doubt if she did, he would quickly work out some plausible excuse for Alex. LJ and her parents had a lot in common.

'Think over what I've said,' LJ pleaded as he said goodbye, and Sara kissed his cheek without answering.

She didn't know if his version was the truth or not—but even if he had been telling the truth, even if Alex hadn't had an affair with Madeleine, it didn't alter anything. Sara was still angry at having been asked to trust Alex implicitly without a word from him.

Alex had been testing her, had he? How dared he ask her to prove her love after four years of happy marriage? She had allowed him to turn her into something approaching a slave, but that hadn't been enough for him. It hadn't sated his craving for power over her. He had wanted more; demanded that she believe what he told her to believe, think what he told her to think. Alex had denied her any free will, flung her an ultimatum— accept my word or leave me.

What else could she have done? She wondered wryly about LJ's wife—was Leah Jonas the sort of woman who would let her husband do her thinking for her? Was that why Alex expected as much from Sara? She knew how closely he had modelled himself on LJ—the older man had had a deep influence on him, he had been the only father figure in Alex's life.

Walking back into the kitchen she found her parents busy making a salad for lunch; her father crisply dicing pepper while her mother washed lettuce at the sink. They looked around, smiling. 'Has Mr Jonas gone? A pity he couldn't stay for lunch, he's such a charming man, so easy to talk to,' her mother said.

'He's a clever one,' Sara said drily. LJ had soon wheedled her mother into doing whatever he asked. Charm was a dangerous weapon.

She spent the afternoon sunbathing in the garden, in a bikini, occasionally skimming over a few pages of a book she was reading. After an early supper she went up to bed, feeling that it had been a very long day. LJ's visit had exhausted her. The evenings lasted for hours at that time of the year, the light died reluctantly in the warm sky and the birds were noisy until well after ten o'clock at night. Sara fell asleep with that haunting sound echoing in her ears; the flutter of wings, the melancholy call of the birds.

It reminded her too much of the years when she went to sleep with the whisper and sigh of the sea in her ears; at first she had found it so hard to sleep in London, she had missed the customary lullaby of the tide. Now, though, she found the night time ebb and flow of London traffic an acceptable substitute; from a distance it made an oddly similar sound.

She ate a late breakfast and sunbathed again for an hour after ringing her boss and giving him a personal explanation of her absence.

'Don't even think of hurrying back!' he ordered. 'We want you with your brains intact, you're no good to us without your head.'

Sara laughed as she rang off. She had been very lucky to land that job, it had been a sheer fluke that she turned out to have a flair for writing advertising copy. You had to have a certain sort of mind, quick and inventive; and a sense of humour helped, too. Sara didn't feel she had much sense of humour at the moment. Alex had dented it.

Her father had gone back to work. He had several assistants, perfectly capable of running the shop without him, but he had the sort of mind that prefers routine. It disturbed him to alter his habits, and he couldn't help believing that when he wasn't there the place fell to pieces without him.

Sara felt she had had enough sun at around eleven-thirty and collected up her possessions to go back indoors. Her mother was in the kitchen, shelling peas.

'I'll do those for you,' Sara offered at once,

pleased to have something to occupy her, and her mother cheerfully let her take over.

Mrs Calthrop looked at the round-faced kitchen clock, an abstracted expression in her eyes. 'Sara, would you mind if I popped round to the church hall for half an hour? I promised to help sort out the jumble for this weekend's sale but I didn't want to leave you alone, only they're short-handed because Mrs Pomfret has broken her leg and Judy King isn't able to leave little George, he's got the measles and won't stop scratching.'

Sara grinned. 'No need to worry about me, I'm okay. Go ahead.'

Her mother took off her flowered apron, hovering uncertainly. 'I won't be long, I promise.'

'Get off with you,' Sara said, popping a pod noisily and watching the fat green peas rolling into the colander. It was one of those satisfying small experiences that she missed in London, where she bought her peas frozen in packets. Her mother grew most of her own vegetables; there were neat rows of lettuce and carrots, a trellis loaded with growing runner beans and peas, a small herb garden and a large patch of potato plants. Mrs Calthrop bottled her own fruit, too, and made jams with the gooseberries, raspberries, strawberries and other soft fruit she grew. At the back of the garden stood apple and cherry trees which, a month ago, had been covered in blossom.

When her mother had gone the house seemed peaceful and quiet, sunlight made oblongs and rectangles on the floor and Sara didn't hurry with her pea-shelling. It was a pleasant job in this warm light. She was wearing a thin cotton tunic with no sleeves and a low neckline. The jade green colour suited her and the fine material felt light and smooth on her body. She didn't have enough energy to do anything but a quiet, routine task like shelling peas, but she felt relaxed until the doorbell rang abruptly and she jumped into a new mood, her skin cold with nerves.

It was Alex; she knew it. She couldn't face him, she had had enough trauma for this week. She wasn't going to open the door, she was going to keep very quiet and still and hope he would go away.

The bell rang again, longer and louder. Sara dropped the pod she had been holding and which she had twisted into a torn wreck. Peas rolled across the table. She stood up, letting them fall, her nerves prickling.

Why couldn't he leave her alone? Why had her mother gone out and left her? Had her mother let Alex know that she was on her own? Sara closed her eyes, her lips tight. She wouldn't put it past her mother.

What if Alex came round the back of the house? He knew she wouldn't open the door. She leapt to the kitchen door and turned the lock just as she heard the sound of footsteps on the path outside. The kitchen door was mostly glass, she hurriedly began to draw a curtain across it, to hide her from Alex's searching eyes, but as she did so she saw a face stoop and press against the glass, staring in at her, the nose flattened and the eyes round and amazed.

She gave a shuddering sigh of recognition, and fumbled for the key, unlocked the door again and opened it.

'What on earth were you up to?' Peter asked her teasingly as he bent to kiss her. 'Playing hide and seek, darling?'

CHAPTER EIGHT

'YOU'RE very quiet—you're not in any pain, are you, darling?' Peter asked half an hour later as they sat drinking coffee in the sitting-room, and Sara gave a start, glancing at him guiltily.

'No, my head doesn't hurt much any more.' She could hardly tell him that she was quiet because she had rarely thought of him since they last met—in fact, of course, she had literally forgotten his existence for a short while. Peter had been wiped from her memory banks as if he had never entered her life, and that made her uneasy every time she looked at him.

Peter put down his cup, frowning. 'Look, you weren't hurt because I didn't fly back the minute I heard about the accident, were you? I would have come if I had thought you needed me, you know that, don't you, Sara? Your mother told me it was only a scratch, I wasn't to worry about it.' He had turned a dark red as he talked and Sara guessed that he had felt guilty, too. Peter had an uncomfortable conscience; he must have been torn between coming back at once to see how serious the accident was and staying on to complete the business he had gone to Holland to do.

'Of course, I understand—it would have been silly to come back, there was nothing you could do,' she assured him but her voice was the polite tone of a stranger and Peter noticed it, watching her closely.

'But something is wrong,' he insisted shrewdly.

'No, of course not,' she lied because how could she tell him that she had had amnesia, forgotten all about him, gone back to her ex-husband and slept in the same bed with him for a night? Peter would then fire off a string of questions she preferred not to have to answer. Did you have sex with him? would be the first, no doubt, and although she could honestly say she hadn't, what if the second question was: did you want to?

'So you spent three days in hospital?' Peter asked, not quite convinced but accepting her denial.

'I only got out yesterday morning,' she said.

'And the accident was on Sunday afternoon?'

'Yes, when I was on my way back to town. The train crashed just outside Ashford, I told you.' She had already given him a brief version of events.

'Bad luck that you were the only passenger injured.'

'Several other people were in shock, I gather. There was a report of it in the local paper; it's somewhere around. When Mum gets back I'll ask her for it.'

Peter leaned back in his chair, the sunlight glinting on his stolid cheekbones and that smooth blond hair. He closed his eyes and looked tired. He had driven here straight from Heathrow and Sara felt so guilty as she watched him. Poor Peter. She felt as if she hadn't seen him for a hundred years, as if she had never known him in the first place. Over the last five days her life had been moving at a hectic pace, too much had happened too soon, she was in a state of anguished confusion, and Peter didn't fit into this scattered jigsaw puzzle which was her life. He was a spare piece, from another puzzle. She had convinced herself he would fit but he was entirely the wrong shape, colour and pattern.

Looking back to Saturday when she left London to be at the anniversary lunch she wished desperately that she had changed her mind and gone to Amsterdam with Peter as he asked. None of this would have happened, then. She wouldn't have seen Alex again, she wouldn't have turned over the stone and uncovered all the hidden twistings and turnings of her own psyche that she had blocked off from the light a year ago.

'Did you ever get down to the cottage? Is it up for sale?' Peter asked casually.

She jumped. 'What?'

He stared at her flushed face. 'You were going to check to see if Stevenson had put it on the market, don't you remember?' He shrugged his broad shoulders. 'Well, never mind, your accident must have driven it out of your mind. Look, why don't I go and take a look at the place now?'

'No,' Sara said urgently, trembling, then stammered: 'It isn't up for sale.'

Peter was on his feet. He looked down at her, frowning. 'What does he think he's playing at? The man is a nuisance. I've a good mind to go and see him, force him to see sense.'

'No,' Sara said again with even more nervous force. 'Don't do that, Peter.' She hated to picture that interview. Peter had no idea what sort of man he was dealing with—he would get the shock of his life if he did tackle Alex in person.

Staring at him, Sara realised that she had unconsciously—or was it consciously?—picked a man who was the absolute opposite of Alex in every way. Peter was calm to the point of being phlegmatic, he was gentle to the point of being colourless, he was domesticated and house-trained and a stranger to the darker regions of passion. Emotion embarrassed him, he distrusted desire, he wanted a life as placid and neat as the sort of garden he would have; with billiard-table green lawns and unblemished flower beds in which no weeds grew.

'I think I ought to,' Peter insisted. 'What's his London address? Is he there at the moment?'

'I don't know,' Sara said desperately. She suspected Alex was still at the cottage but he hadn't been in touch while she was in the hospital; she didn't know exactly what he was doing. Perhaps he had gone back to London after LJ left?

'When are you coming back to London?' Peter asked, staring at her with faintly puzzled eyes.

'In a few days—the hospital want me to go back there to have these stitches out and I'm not supposed to start work again until after that.'

'You're in a strange mood,' Peter said, looking bewildered, poor man. 'You don't seem the same girl. I suppose it's this crack on the head. Funny how illness changes people.'

She laughed weakly. 'Isn't it?' He had no idea how ironic the words were—her head injury had certainly changed her, quite drastically. She felt like a weather vane after a stormy night; she had blown violently one way and then back again in far too short a time. She was completely disorientated, she no longer knew what she wanted or in which direction she was really pointing.

There was an apprehensive look in Peter's eyes. Was he wondering whether he had been wise in deciding to marry a girl with such a very different temperament? She had subdued her behaviour to match what she sensed Peter wanted over the past months, but you can't suppress your real nature for long and although Sara was basically a domesticated creature she was also a deeply emotional one and her reactions could be too extreme for Peter's placid nature. She looked back at him uneasily. Would he give her the emotional security she needed? Or would he expect her to be self-contained and self-possessed, like himself?

Mrs Calthrop got back a few moments later. As she came into the room and saw Peter her face changed; a surprised and not exactly delighted expression coming into it.

'Oh,' she said and Sara silently raged at her tone. 'Oh, hallo, Peter, how are you?' Her voice made it clear she couldn't care less how he was and Sara resented her insulting courtesy.

'I'm very well, Mrs Calthrop—how are you?' Peter responded with almost as little enthusiasm. They talked like remote acquaintances and always would. Her parents would never accept Peter and he was indifferent to their off-handed manner. It wasn't simply that her parents loved Alex, but there was something about Peter himself that they didn't like, although Sara couldn't fathom what it was about him that put that look in their eyes, but she saw that if she married Peter she was going to find herself increasingly cut off from her family.

She frowned, disturbed, and her mother said at once: 'How's your head, Sara?'

Peter looked concerned. 'She isn't at all well, is she, Mrs Calthrop?' he said. 'I was just saying— she isn't the same girl at the moment. I should never have left her alone while I went to Holland.'

Mrs Calthrop looked at her daughter shrewdly and Sara felt herself going pink. Her mother guessed that Sara hadn't told Peter about her amnesia, the hours she had spent alone with Alex. There was curiosity and a faint teasing in Mrs Calthrop's eyes; she was amused by Sara's flush.

Peter stood by the window, looking out. 'Lovely countryside around here,' he said. 'Very quiet, isn't it? I don't know if I'd like that. I'm a city boy.' He laughed, looking round at them, and Sara forced a smile but she felt her stomach clench in apprehension. She had learnt how to live in a city but she had been born and grown up here on the wind-swept marsh, and her eyes often ached for the level green fields and rainy vistas she still saw inwardly while she was walking through canyoned streets.

'You must show Peter the village while he's here,' Mrs Calthrop suggested. 'It's quite a tourist spot in summer; the houses are very picturesque, Peter. I'm sure you'd like it.'

'That sounds a good idea,' Peter said, looking at his watch. 'I have to drive back to town tonight, though, I'm afraid I have an important appointment tomorrow.'

'I'll get lunch now and then you'll still have time to spend a few hours with Sara,' Mrs Calthrop said, making an effort to be friendly. It was a pity her struggle showed. Peter's gaze followed her wryly as she went out of the room.

'Your mother isn't too keen on me, is she?' he said.

'She hasn't really got to know you very well,' Sara evaded.

That afternoon she and Peter drove into the village and parked close to the White Abbas church, got out and strolled around the church-yard, went into the twelfth-century building to admire a faded brass commemorating a local crusader and a few dusty, ragged banners brought back from the Napoleonic wars by one of the squire's sons who had fought under Wellington and survived the battle of Waterloo. White Abbas had never entered the history books, no great men had lived there, no battles had been fought in the area. It had an air of comfortable placidity which Sara felt Peter should appreciate, but under that ran a wilder vein. While the squire's son was fighting the French the men of White Abbas were happily engaged in secret trade with them—smugglers had always inhabited the marsh, it was a countryside which was ideal for them and the coastline was so close to the coast of France. Brandy had been run into the marsh and taken by hidden ways across the misty, hedge-enclosed fields to lie in caches in churchyards like this one or buried deep among the hay in some remote barn.

'Smugglers?' Peter said, making a distasteful face. 'You know, I've never seen anything romantic in them, they were criminals, nasty ones, too. They didn't just smuggle contraband, they killed anyone who got in their way. An unpleasant collection.'

Sara sighed. He was probably right, but she preferred her own view of the darker side of marsh history. She followed him out of the shadowy interior of the church, listening to him admiring the stained glass windows.

'They're only Victorian,' she pointed out. 'The originals were smashed by Cromwell's men.' The new ones had solemn angels and worthy sentiments, very Victorian.

'Now Cromwell is someone I do admire,' Peter said enthusiastically.

'I might have known you would,' Sara said. She detested Oliver Cromwell and the Puritans, she was vehemently on the side of King Charles, just as she found the stained-glass smugness of the Victorian windows distinctly less beautiful than the mellow, crumbling stone and soaring arches of the older part of the church.

Peter smiled indulgently at her. 'You're a romantic,' he said, a statement she easily translated as: 'you're a poor simpleton, my love, but you can't help it.'

'Yes, I am,' she said defiantly, her chin up and her green eyes sharp.

Peter walked around the mossy churchyard, watching the sheep with a touch of disapproval. 'Should they be in here wandering over the graves?'

'They keep the grass cropped and the village can't afford a full-time gardener,' Sara said. 'It's ecology,' she added vaguely.

'What on earth are you talking about?' Peter said, sounding irritated. 'Do you know?'

'Yes, I know,' Sara snapped. 'It means that the sheep like it and we like it so mind your own business.' She loved the village, it was her home, it made her furious to hear it being criticised.

A fast silver car shot past and Sara stiffened as she unlatched the church gate and walked through it. Every silver car she saw wasn't going to belong to Alex, but seeing it had made her nervous, especially at that moment. She knew that she and Peter were on the verge of squabbling, something they had never done before.

Why were they clashing so much now? she wondered, kicking a stone in a sulky, childish way. Was it because she was on edge after what had recently happened? Her head wound might be making her irritable. But she knew it was more worrying than that—everything Peter said or did was making her prickle with impatience and that wasn't fair to him. He hadn't changed, he was the man she had been so sure she wanted a week ago. Any shift of feeling had been inside her.

She had been on the rebound from Alex when

she met Peter and she had liked in Peter the very
things which now irritated her. Those slow, calm,
conservative qualities which made him a good
businessman, a reliable husband for anyone, had
been what she thought she wanted and were now
what made her teeth clench.

She felt even more guilty as Peter put his arm
round her and smiled at her. 'Sorry I was a cross-
patch,' she murmured, leaning her head against
him.

'You're not yourself,' he said soothingly, but
that was the whole trouble, Sara realised. She
hadn't been herself during the past year, she had
been searching desperately for some stability
after her break-up with Alex, but the self Peter
was seeing today was the Sara she had been
trying to bury for ever. It was the woman he had
known who had been a false image—the real one
was the Sara he couldn't recognise and didn't
understand.

They stood outside the lych gate in the shadow
of a great oak. When Sara looked into Peter's face
it was placid and unaware of the turmoil going on
inside her head. He bent to kiss her lightly.
'Don't look so upset, you get too emotional,' he
said as if she were a child.

At that moment she heard another car and shot
a look sideways to catch the gleam of silver—the
car she had seen a moment ago must have turned
and come back. Her heart flipped over and she
took a deep breath. Oh, no! she thought, taking a
quick second look as the silver car pulled to a
sudden halt. It can't be! she assured herself, but
it was, of course. She saw Alex uncoiling his long

body from behind the steering wheel, he stood up
and slammed the car door before striding towards
them.

Peter had never seen him before, but the
village high street was so empty and peaceful that
any other sign of human life was interesting, so
he looked curiously at Alex, recognising him as
someone else who did not fit among these
dreaming surroundings. Alex might only be
wearing black jeans and a black sweater, but the
jeans were obviously designer made and the
sweater was undoubtedly cashmere. As he walked
rapidly across the road Sara saw the soft folds
cling to his lean body and knew he was wearing
nothing under the cashmere. The sweater's deep
v-neck revealed brown skin, a glimpse of his bare
shoulder. She swallowed nervously, half inclined
to grab Peter's hand and run for it.

Peter would be amazed if she suggested it,
though. She gave him a wry, sideways look,
sighing. It would offend Peter's dignity, it might
make him inconveniently suspicious, it would
unquestionably give Alex a good deal of amusement, and that was the real reason why Sara
didn't try it.

'Sightseeing?' Alex enquired and Peter
imagined he was talking to him, he gave him a
politely friendly smile, nodding, although he was
a little taken aback to be addressed by a total
stranger.

'Yes, it's a pretty village, isn't it?'

Alex's brows rose steeply, he looked Peter up
and down in a cool assessment which made Sara
flush. She did not like the gleam which entered

those bright, catlike eyes. Alex looked far too
satisfied by what he saw; Peter's bland manner,
his conservative blue suit and striped blue and
white shirt, his well-brushed blond hair and
firmly fleshed face.

'Now who are you, I wonder?' Alex drawled
but before Peter could answer his eyes had
switched disconcertingly to Sara and he added
with a curl of his lips: 'The boyfriend, I
presume?'

Her colour deepened and her hands screwed up
into fists as she stared angrily back at him,
wishing she dared punch him on that supercilious
long nose.

'Just watch it!' she threatened hoarsely and felt
Peter's start of shocked surprise at her tone.

'Or what?' Alex mocked challengingly. He was
enjoying this and Sara's eyes hated him, a fact of
which he was well aware and to which he was
tormentingly indifferent. The angrier she became,
the more Alex would enjoy himself, so Sara
struggled to hold on to her temper.

'Peter, this is . . .' she began and Alex interrupted coolly.

'Her husband.' That was not how she had
intended to introduce him—she had meant
merely to tell Peter his name, she felt her spine
prickle at the carefully delivered possessive
phrasing.

Peter was no fool, he had already begun to
suspect Alex's identity, and had slowly flushed a
moment ago when it dawned on him. He
managed to pull himself together, though, and
held out his hand with a stiffly polite smile.

'How do you do? I'm Peter Mallory.'

Alex regarded his hand indifferently, pushing his own hands into the back pockets of his jeans, the lazy posture of his body somehow silently insulting. After a second or two Peter let his hand drop, even more flushed but hanging on to his smile in the teeth of Alex's deliberate provocation.

'I've been intending to suggest a meeting sometime soon. This is very opportune.'

Alex gave him an incredulous stare, arching his brows. 'Is it?'

'Don't you think it was time we met? I mean, we're all civilised people and we do have a great deal to discuss, don't we?'

'Do we?' Alex enquired with an air of encouragement which made Sara's nerves flicker wildly. She didn't trust him in this mood, in any mood, but especially not in this one.

'Perhaps we could meet in more relaxed surroundings?' Peter ploughed on, convinced that he could talk Alex into seeing the sense of talking the problem out. 'Have lunch, talk matters over like two sane men?'

Alex laughed and looked mockingly at Sara. 'Does he always talk like that?'

'Oh, shut up!' she muttered, feeling Peter stiffening, but it wasn't Alex's taunting that had enraged Peter it was something else he had just noticed—a small boy coolly try to start Peter's car. They hadn't locked the doors. It hadn't seemed necessary in the quiet little village. Peter gave a howl of rage and ran towards his car and Alex stared after him with dry amusement.

'You haven't told him, have you?' he drawled, suddenly turning his head to look down at her. Sara's eyes slid away from the probe of his stare. She didn't answer.

'He isn't going to like it much when he finally discovers that you've slept with me again,' Alex said softly, and her eyes spat fire at him.

'In the same bed but not . . .'

'Not what?' he asked wickedly as she came to a stop, flushing vividly.

'You know what I mean,' she snapped.

'Sex?' he queried in dulcet tones. 'We didn't have sex? Well, that's strictly true, but I bet we came closer than you've ever come with him.' He was watching her intently, alert to every shade of expression in her face. 'You haven't slept with him, have you, Sara?'

'Oh, you can tell, can you?' she threw at him bitterly, and he gave her an odd, brooding look, nodding.

'I can tell. It was obvious while you were at the cottage with me.'

Her face burned, knowing he was right—she had needed his passion and hadn't even tried to hide the fact. How could she have betrayed herself like that?

Peter was chasing the little boy away, threatening to box his ears if he came back. As soon as he was out of range of Peter's long arms, the boy turned and danced up and down making insulting gestures, yelling rude names, then shot off as Peter began to come after him.

Red with temper, Peter came back towards them. Alex surveyed him with smiling contempt.

'You are out of your mind, my darling,' he said to her. 'You can't really want a pompous idiot like that. Who are you trying to kid?'

Peter heard enough to look belligerently at him as he joined them. 'I don't like your tone,' he told Alex coldly and Alex laughed, baring his teeth charmingly.

'I don't like your suit, but I was too polite to say so.'

'I don't find you amusing,' Peter snapped, even angrier. He hated being laughed at.

'No sense of humour, either, eh?' Alex noted, looking at Sara. 'Would you call him a bargain? He's no oil painting and I suspect his brains are in his cheque-book.'

Hectically flushed, Peter snarled at him. 'You know what you're asking for, don't you?'

'I know what *you're* going to get,' Alex smiled and Peter bristled from head to toe like an angry dog.

'Let's go home, Peter,' Sara said desperately, taking his hand, but he shook her off as if she were a buzzing insect, without even looking at her, too intent on outstaring Alex to notice her, and Sara stumbled and almost fell.

'Don't push my wife around,' Alex said through his teeth, glancing at her with a frown. 'Sara, go and sit down. You shouldn't be standing around in this heat.'

'You won't get away with threatening me,' Peter said, scowling.

'I'll deal with you in a minute,' Alex told him, taking Sara's waist between both hands and lifting her on to the churchyard wall. 'Sit there and keep cool,' he told her as she glared at him impotently.

'Alex, you're not to hurt him,' she said, clutching at his shoulder. He gave her a glinting smile.

'I don't like his face,' he explained. 'I'm just going to re-arrange it a little.'

She drummed her heels on the churchyard wall. 'Alex!' But he was already walking away and Peter had overheard what they said and been infuriated, not surprisingly. He was measuring Alex's lean body with eyes that misread the long-limbed grace as less powerful than his own stocky build. With a snarl he lunged aggressively but his blow didn't connect. Alex moved too fast, weaving to one side, and darting forward a second later to punch Peter in the jaw. Sara winced, hearing the crunch of bone on bone and Peter's gasp of pain.

Alex rubbed his knuckles, grimacing. 'That hurt me as much as it did you,' he said, grinning.

Peter didn't find that funny, either. He had blood behind his eyes, his face contorted with rage as he hurled himself back at Alex.

She crouched against the churchyard wall in the shadow of the gently shifting oak tree boughs, watching them bitterly. What did they think they were proving? She wasn't the only audience they had now—a small ginger cat had emerged from a gate and was sitting on the other side of the road, watching with fascination. It lifted one paw and began to clean itself without taking its green eyes off the men's struggling figures. In the house from which it had obviously just come a curtain twitched and a face showed at the window, eyes amazed. Sara put her hands over her face, groaning. This would be all round the village tomorrow—all round the whole marsh, come to that.

Peter reeled back and sat down suddenly, his blond hair dishevelled. Sara looked at him dispassionately and without sympathy. He had pushed her aside when she tried to stop him fighting. Peter hadn't fought Alex over her—he had resented the way Alex spoke to him, that was all. It was his own ego he had been fighting for, not Sara, and, anyway, who asked him to fight at all? Men were such fools.

Alex straightened, breathing hard, and pulled his sweater down where Peter's clutching hands had rumpled it. He raked his hair back, glancing at her, and Sara eyed him resentfully.

'You want to marry *him*?' Alex asked bitingly.

Sara considered a number of replies, but none of them seemed the right one. 'Yes,' she said at last because she wanted to take the complacent smile off his face, and it certainly did that. He looked at her with hard, narrowed eyes, and she got down from the wall and turned away with what she hoped appeared to be cool disdain.

She meant to go over to Peter and help him up, wipe the blood from his cheek with her handkerchief, but she only took one step. The next second Alex's hands grabbed her and slung her over his shoulder in a fireman's lift.

She didn't believe it was happening for a few seconds, and Alex strode across the road before she reacted. By the time Sara began kicking and yelling she was too late. Mid-scream, she was deposited ruthlessly into the passenger seat and in the brief time it took her to gather her wits together and understand what he was going to do Alex had got into the car beside her. Sara had turned to fumble with the door handle, Alex leant across and slapped her hand away.

'Naughty!'

'Bastard,' Sara screeched, beside herself with fury now. Peter struggled to his feet, a hand to his swelling jaw, and the little ginger cat sat up with alert ears and front paws together, the oriental gaze of his bright eyes riveted on the car, looking for all the world like a miniature Sphinx with the white dust of an English road substituting for lone and level sands.

'Where did you learn such language?' Alex reproved, starting the engine.

'I'm not going anywhere with you,' she assured him, grabbing for the door handle again as a small boy on a bicycle wobbled round the corner and almost fell off in amazement when Peter lurched across the road right in front of the bike.

'He should look where he's going,' Alex criticised Peter, as he grabbed Sara's wrist and forced it down while he dangerously accelerated with just one hand on the wheel.

'You'll kill us both,' she wailed, cowering in her seat as the car shot away. The woman at the cottage window had her nose pressed against the pane now, abandoning any pretence of discretion, her rounded eyes agog.

In the driving mirror Sara saw Peter come to a breathless halt, staring after them in the very middle of the road. An oncoming car almost hit him and he leapt to one side while Sara watched, horror-struck.

'How could you?' she spat at Alex, turning on him, her face white now and her auburn hair blowing around her face in tangled coils, as the wind tore through the speeding car. 'What the hell do you think you're doing? I hate you! Do you hear me, Alex? I hate you!'

He glanced at her through his lashes, his mouth crooked with a bitter humour, and shrugged. 'I was only taking what was mine in the first place.'

'Not any more,' she said hoarsely, angry with herself at the fierce shudder that went through her. 'It doesn't matter what you do—I'm still divorcing you.'

CHAPTER NINE

'DAMN!' Alex said and she looked at him quickly, her eyes wary, but it wasn't her insistence that she hated him that had made him swear. His gaze was fixed on the driving mirror and his mouth was impatient. 'He's coming after us!' he added and Sara turned to look over her shoulder, startled and alarmed.

Peter's car was coming after them at a speed that made her blink; it wasn't like Peter to drive too fast, he was normally the most cautious and law-abiding driver in the world, but he was unquestionably breaking the speed limit at the moment and she could see from the hunched way he crouched at the wheel that he was in a ferocious temper. Sara had never seen Peter in a temper before; she hadn't thought he had it in him, this was a new Peter she was seeing and she bit her lip, thinking that it was time she stopped being so sure she could read character. She had thought she knew Alex and he had taught her she was wrong. Now Peter was acting out of the character she had cast him as—or was he?

Whenever she saw Peter he was gentle, calm, polite, indulgent—but that couldn't be how he was at work. He wouldn't hold down a high-powered job by being gentle and polite and the solid lines of his face had suggested an aggression which certainly fitted the way he had hurled himself at Alex a few minutes ago. Grimly she recognised that she was seeing the side of Peter he suppressed when he was with her. If she had glimpsed it when they first met, she would never have dated him. It had been his difference from Alex that attracted her; she was only now realising that Peter had things in common with Alex, too.

'I'll have to shake him off,' Alex decided with unhidden glee, twisting the wheel to the left and spinning into a narrow lane bordered by high hedges.

'What are you doing?' gasped Sara. 'This isn't a game of cops and robbers! Don't be so stupid!' She watched, thunderstruck, as Peter's car screamed after them, taking the corner on three wheels.

'People in glass houses shouldn't throw stones,' Alex told her gnomically, baffling her for a moment until she had thought that out and decided she was offended.

'*I'm* not stupid!' She glanced back again and saw that Peter's car was gaining on them. Alex saw it, too, and put his foot down on the accelerator, shooting past a field gate just as a tractor was about to turn out in front of him. The tractor driver leapt about, galvanised, shaking his fists after Alex before he slowly drew out in front of Peter. Sara flinched, taking a wild gasp of air, but Peter's brakes must have been good, he slewed across the road and landed with the nose of the car in a ditch, missing the tractor by inches.

'You lunatic!' she shouted at Alex who was

watching the whole scene in his driving mirror and grinning. 'You could have killed one of them!'

'I was not driving your boyfriend's car—he was! If he wanted to drive dangerously in a narrow country road, that was his problem.' Alex slowed down and turned sedately into a lane leading down to the sea road.

'Peter never drives like that normally. It was your fault,' she gabbled angrily. 'You needled him into driving like that.'

'He shouldn't lose his temper,' Alex drawled and she trembled with rage at his self-satisfied smile. Ever since Alex walked across the road towards them outside the church he had been cold-bloodedly nudging Peter into a brawl, but he, himself, had never lost his cool. He had known exactly what he was doing throughout; he had summed Peter up in two seconds flat and seen the subterranean belligerence that Sara had missed, not simply recognised it but known how to shatter Peter's outward calm and provoke that temper. Alex had quick, sharp intuitions about people. He must have picked up both Peter's dislike of losing his temper and in consequence his self-control; and also the precise way of snapping Peter's usual hold on the temper he found so embarrassing. Having seen all that, Alex hadn't had a qualm about using his guesswork. He had played poor Peter like a bewildered bull, gracefully circling him, waving a red cape, until Peter charged.

'You're despicable,' Sara seethed, then saw where they were heading and sat up stiffly in the passenger seat. 'I'm not going to the cottage with you! Take me home.' She turned to glare at him. 'Do you hear? I won't go to the cottage.'

Alex didn't bother to answer, he drove down the sea road, his eyes on the clear blue horizon where a tanker was steaming slowly through the Channel. The sea had a millpond placidity today, not a wave seemed to break the surface, there were no white caps to betray wind velocity and the shore was busy with feeding plovers, their black-ringed necks dipping as they searched for molluscs among the wet sand.

'Did you hear me?' Sara repeated, watching the taut edge of his profile with far too much intensity.

He pulled up outside the cottage and Sara at once opened her door and almost fell out. She walked away from him quickly down to the beach. The tide had drained away, leaving the usual litter of torn weed, shells and driftwood. Sara was wearing flat summer shoes with rope soles which left behind a trail of footprints the damp sand retained.

The plovers took fright and scattered, making off to the further end of the beach. Sara paused to stare out over the glinting, milky water, aware that Alex was right behind her. He didn't try to touch her, he merely came to a halt beside her, inches away, the quiet level sound of his breathing louder than the murmur of the sea.

'I didn't have an affair with Madeleine,' he said with the same insistent obstinacy he had shown a year ago. 'Perhaps if I go on saying it until we're both ninety, you'll begin to believe me.'

Sara folded her arms across her breast in an unconscious gesture of self-defence, shivering as if she were cold, although the day was still warm and languid.

'I believe you,' she said flatly because LJ had convinced her, as much by his own unquestioning belief as by what he told her about Madeleine's pursuit of Alex.

She felt Alex staring at her averted face, was aware of tension in the way he stood there, his lean body motionless yet poised.

'You do?' he questioned with an unusual uncertainty, and for once she could read his mind without difficulty. He had seen the obstacle between them very simply as her refusal to accept his word that he hadn't had an affair with his secretary, and perhaps in the beginning it had been that simple, but it had rapidly become far deeper, more complex, when Alex tried to railroad her into accepting his unsupported word. He might be right in wanting her to trust him that implicitly, perhaps perfect love is perfect trust, but Sara was miserably aware of her own human imperfection and her need for conviction and certainty.

When Alex refused to explain what lay behind Matt Bentley's accusations, he was putting her on trial, and Sara resented the demands he was making on her love. If he had told her what LJ had told her yesterday, she would have believed him. If he had said: 'I'm having Madeleine transferred to another office because she's chasing me and it is becoming embarrassing,' she wouldn't have doubted his word, in spite of what

Matt Bentley had told her. The real wedge which had been driven between them had been Alex's refusal to tell her anything, his flat insistence that she simply accept his word and hold her tongue. Prove you love me, Alex had demanded, but he hadn't been proving his love for her. He had let her leave him, ignored her for months, while he sulked because she wouldn't slavishly do as he wished. Alex had expected such total abnegation of self because he didn't love her. No human being had the right to expect another to love like that. You don't have to reason with a dog. You say: 'Stay' and the dog stays. You say 'Go' and the dog goes and never asks why. But a woman isn't a dog and she does ask why when she is given an unreasonable demand.

'It doesn't make any difference now,' Sara said sadly and Alex caught her shoulders and spun her to face him, staring down at her.

'What the hell does that mean? Doesn't make any difference? What has all this been about?'

'Love,' Sara said with dry melancholy and felt his fingers tighten on her flesh, the tips embedding themselves in her upper arm.

'Don't try to tell me you're in love with that guy I just knocked to kingdom come, because I don't believe it. He's not your type, even your parents see that. You wouldn't be happy with him, he'd make you live in some suburban bungalow with plaster gnomes in the garden and an endless vista of television aerials to look at. You're a country girl, you couldn't breathe in London.'

'It doesn't matter where you live as long as

you're happy!' Sara looked at him neutrally, untouched now by the brooding intensity with which his golden eyes hunted over her face, probing the remoteness she wore, looking for a chink in that armour and baffled by her mood.

'You wouldn't be happy with him!'

'Perhaps not,' she admitted calmly. She had managed to convince herself she would be, but she knew now why she had clung to Peter for months and she felt guilty about the way she had used him, however unknowingly. She had needed his support and wound around him like bindweed, but that weakness was in the past and she would never use anyone again, any more than she would consent to be used.

Alex's face relaxed slightly, his hands slid over her slender shoulders, caressing, coaxing. Sara looked at him without expression; he was still trying to manipulate her, pull her strings and make her move to his command in a puppet show of his invention. His love had no depth, no reality, because for Alex she did not exist as a three-dimensional woman with a mind and separate life of her own.

'But I wouldn't be happy with you, either,' she added.

She saw the flash of his eyes without alarm. Alex didn't frighten her any more; he never would again. She had understood herself and in doing so had begun to understand him. He could only frighten her if she loved him weakly, helplessly, without getting back an equal love from him. Alex had come into her life while she was too young; he had dropped out of the sky like a marauding eagle and carried her off in his talons. He had possessed her and she hadn't dreamt of escaping, she had abandoned herself to captivity as if it was joy—and while she was in that bondage of desire she had been afraid, of him, of herself. Afraid of losing him, of failing him, of displeasing him—and the more she trembled and gave in to him the harsher became the tyranny of what Alex called his love for her.

'That's a lie!' he snarled, his jaw tightening. 'You were happy with me until you started doubting me.'

'I was living in a fool's paradise. My eyes were opened.'

'I don't know what the hell you're talking about,' he said with rough impatience. 'You just told me that you believed I hadn't had an affair with Madeleine.'

'Forget about her, she really wasn't important, she was just the straw that broke the camel's back. I left you because of her but it wasn't until I got away from you that it dawned on me what a fool I'd been for years.'

His brows met, a hard black line above his watchful eyes. 'Are you suggesting that there had been other women before . . .'

'No, that wasn't what I meant,' she said flatly. Where was the point of trying to explain it to him? He wouldn't understand, he would only try to coerce her because force was the only language that he did understand. In his own way, Alex loved her—or, at least, needed her. The tyrant needs his slaves; without them he can't exist, his need is greater than theirs.

'Then what did you mean? Stop being so enigmatic, talk to me, explain . . .' his brusque voice stopped dead as she looked up at him drily, her face sardonic.

'You were saying?'

Alex looked startled, his eyes narrowing. He didn't answer and Sara smiled with derision at him.

'You sounded like an echo,' she said. 'That's what I said to you a year ago—explain, I begged you. Talk to me, tell me what this is all about. And what did you say, Alex? Don't ask questions, you said, don't press me for explanations. Just accept what I'm telling you, my word is final.'

Above them on the sea road they suddenly heard the roar of an engine and then the whine of tyres burning rubber as a car skidded to a halt. Sara looked away from Alex's frowning face to throw a quick glance up the beach to where Peter was leaping out of his car.

'He's caught up with you,' she said.

'Don't you have that wrong? Isn't it you he's after?' Alex said with a sort of tired amusement, and she shook her head.

'No, it isn't my blood he wants. It's yours. Peter's weak spot is his dignity and you hurt him in it.'

She watched Peter running towards them across the sand; the plovers flew up into the air, agitated by this new intrusion into their feeding time, and some gulls shrieked as they soared away on effortless white wings, their black shadows thrown on to the mirror surface of the sea.

'But I might as well take him away,' Sara

thought aloud. 'There's no point in any more fighting and I have some apologising to do.' She swivelled to walk away and Alex caught her elbow, his grip urgent.

'No, Sara! Don't go with him.'

She heard the note of pleading in his voice with painful satisfaction. Alex had shed his arrogance at last, his face was uncertain, he was looking at her and trying to see her, the woman who had matured out of the young girl he had married, the Sara he had never really met. Alex had finally realised that she was not the same Sara who had left his bed a year ago. So much had happened to her while they were apart; the unhappiness of their broken marriage had changed her. She had grown, put out tendrils of feeling and thought, discovered that she could stand alone, begun to understand herself and see what damage had been done to her by allowing Alex to treat her as a household pet.

She gave him a cool look. 'Let go of me, Alex,' she said and she wasn't just referring to the hand gripping her arm, her tone made that crystal clear and Alex got the message. His face was harsh and pale as he watched her, but after a second he released her arm and Sara walked away from him with her dancing shadow running ahead on the wet sand, feeling Alex watching her, immobile where she had left him.

She met Peter half way. He would have run right past her, furiously intent on catching up with Alex, if Sara hadn't stopped him by blocking his path. He almost fell over and gave her a flushed, aggressive glare.

'I'll talk to you later,' he said through his teeth. 'First I've got a few matters to settle with that bastard.'

'Don't waste your time,' Sara said. 'He doesn't fight fair. You may be tough, Peter, but he's in a class of his own. He doesn't intend to lose, no matter what he has to do to make sure of it.'

Peter bristled. 'I don't intend to lose, either, don't count me out before I've given up.'

'I want to talk to you,' Sara said, abandoning that line of persuasion since she saw it had been the wrong one, she had merely exacerbated the situation, made Peter more determined than ever to beat Alex at his own game.

'Later,' Peter said, jaw pugnacious, eyes hard. Sara tried to catch his arm but he strode right past her and with a resigned shrug she let him go and walked back across the beach watching with an odd sense of satisfaction the wavering line of her own footprints leading the way she had come. She carefully did not walk on them, making a neat dual track on the sand. It was a mistake to walk where you had walked before; going back never worked.

Behind her she heard Peter's explosive outburst: 'Right, you bastard! I'll teach you to . . .'

He didn't finish the sentence, nor did Alex speak to him. There was a scuffle and a resounding splash. Sara didn't look round, she walked on with her eyes on the sand, and when she got to the road she went to Peter's car and got into the passenger seat to wait for him.

Alex strode to his car a moment later, got in, slammed the door, started the engine and shot away with a burst of angry noise. Sara glanced down at the beach then and saw Peter padding slowly across the sand, dripping.

She couldn't see his expression at this distance but she didn't need to—she saw the humiliated rage in his every step. She had warned him, but he hadn't listened. She didn't know quite what Alex had done, but she had seen that he was bone dry and apparently undishevelled, every black hair in place, his face unscathed, only the grim set of his shoulders testifying to any reaction to what had happened on the beach. Had he flung Peter over his shoulder with a judo twist? Or merely tripped him up as he ran headlong at him?

She lowered her eyes as Peter got into the driver's seat. His immaculate blue suit was ruined, his feet squelched as he fumbled for the pedals, his blond hair was plastered to his forehead. He started the car without a word, and drove back to her parents' house in total silence.

'You'd better get out of those wet clothes,' Sara said as she got out of the car. 'Have you got your suitcase in the boot? My mother will have your suit cleaned, but you'll need something else to wear if you're going back to London tonight.'

Peter didn't answer. He got out and went to the boot of his car, unlocked it, pulled out a case and set off with it towards the house, leaving damp patches everywhere he went.

Sara bit her lip to stifle a giggle. Poor Peter— he really didn't find anything amusing in the situation and she couldn't blame him. If Alex had hurt his dignity in their first encounter, he had demolished it altogether now, and it didn't help

Peter to say I told you so; it would only make matters worse.

Her mother opened the door, jaw dropping. 'Good heavens, what happened to you?' she asked Peter tactlessly.

'Peter fell into the sea,' Sara intervened quickly. 'Could he have a bath, Mother? He needs to change all his clothes.'

'I should think he does,' Mrs Calthrop said, laughing, and then stopped the laugh as Peter turned morose eyes on her, his chin jowled with resentment. 'Poor man,' she said hurriedly, clucking her tongue. 'Dear, dear. Have you got a change of clothes in your case? Oh, good, well, up you go—it's right in front of you as you turn right on the landing.'

Peter stamped upstairs in what might have been an ominous fashion if his trousers hadn't flapped wetly and his shoes squelched at every step.

Sara fled into the kitchen to hide her head in her hands and laugh. Mrs Calthrop closed the door and joined her, watching her with bemused curiosity.

'What on earth happened?'

Hiccuping, Sara whispered: 'We met Alex.'

Mrs Calthrop sat down. 'Well, go on,' she said impatiently. 'What happened?'

'You saw what happened,' Sara said. 'Alex threw him in the sea.'

'Oh, he didn't?' Mrs Calthrop was torn between amusement and horror.

Sara put her hand over her mouth, shaking with laughter, then sobered abruptly. 'No, it really isn't funny, poor Peter. It wasn't his fault. Alex deliberately provoked a row, he set out to do it from the start. Peter should have walked away and stayed away, but of course he wouldn't, once he had lost his temper there was no stopping him, he rushed on to his destruction.'

'I wish I'd been there,' her mother said wistfully and Sara gave her a scowl.

'Don't think I don't know you don't like Peter!'

'I've never said I didn't like him. Good heavens, I've tried to be very nice to him whenever you've brought him here, I think that's very unfair, Sara.'

'You remember that mongrel dog I brought home when I was in the junior school?' Sara said pointedly. 'The one with fleas who wasn't housetrained? You made me give him back to the girl who'd given him to me, he was only here for one night, but you made him stay in the garden shed and wouldn't let him in the house. Well, that's the way you look at Peter—as though you'd like to shoo him out of the house and make me give him back to wherever I found him.'

Mrs Calthrop looked uncertainly at her. 'Can I help it if I prefer . . .'

'Don't say his name to me!' Sara exploded.

'Sara really! There's no need to shout at me in my own house!' Her mother had flushed with impatience and was eyeing her as though she yearned to smack her, the way she had done when she was small. 'You're becoming very difficult these days. You were a much nicer person when you were with Alex.'

Sara was speechless with rage for a second, then she said with a controlled violence her mother could see in her face although Sara managed to make her voice steady. 'I wasn't a person at all, Mother. I was Alex's wife—aside from that I didn't exist.' She smiled angrily. 'Except from time to time as your daughter— what was it you said to me on my wedding day? Do you remember, Mother? You kissed me and said: "You'll always be my little girl," and that was what you and Alex wanted me to be for the rest of my life. A little girl playing at house, playing at being a wife, playing at being a daughter. But I'm not a little girl and I'm not playing any more. I'm an adult woman and I want to be treated as one.'

Mrs Calthrop sat staring, her mouth open and her eyes stunned. She did not appear to have anything to say, so Sara turned and walked out of the room without feeling she needed to add anything, either.

Peter came downstairs in a very formal pinstriped suit twenty minutes later. Sara had the feeling, as she looked quickly at him, that he had dressed to re-establish his self-respect; even his tie was opulent, a very grave dove grey silk. Peter looked like a man on his dignity, not to be trifled with, ready to take umbrage at the slightest thing.

'We have to talk,' Sara said quietly. 'Come into the sitting-room, please. Can I get you a drink? Some dry sherry?' It seemed appropriate and Peter obviously thought so too because he nodded, sitting down like a mourner at his own funeral.

Sara poured him a generous glass of her

father's best sherry and took a smaller glass for herself. She was going to need it as much as Peter did.

She sat down, nursing her glass, her feet neatly together and her posture decorous to match Peter's sombre mood.

'I'm very sorry, Peter, but . . .'

'Do you really think I need to be told what you're going to say?' he asked sharply. 'I'm not a fool, in fact I'm rather good at mathematics. I don't need to count on my fingers to work out what has happened.'

Sara gave a faint sigh. 'I made a mistake but it was an honest one—I'm very fond of you, I thought we could be happy together, but . . .'

'But now you're going back to your husband!' Peter finished for her, and Sara made a wry face.

'It isn't that. But I've realised that I don't want to get married again—it's too soon, I should have known I was on the rebound when I met you.'

'Thank you,' Peter said, lifting his glass to his lips and swallowing half the sherry in one long gulp. 'I thought you loved me, and that was *my* mistake. I knew something was wrong the minute I walked in here today. You looked horrified to see me.'

'Oh, Peter, I'm . . .'

'Don't say you're sorry, please!' he said irritably. 'I couldn't stand that. If you have any sense, though, you won't go back to that vicious bastard—I don't know what you ever saw in him but women seem to love that macho type, God knows why. I suppose they have a primitive streak.' He finished his sherry and put down the glass, rising. 'There's no point in dragging this out, I'd better go now.'

She followed him unhappily to the door, not knowing what to say to him. He picked up his suitcase in the hall and said stiffly: 'Say goodbye to your mother for me.'

'Peter, just let me say . . .' she began and he scowled. Peter was offended by her sympathy; he wanted no apology, she would only be rubbing salt into the injury she had done him.

'There's no need to have my clothes cleaned,' he said practically. 'I've packed them into a plastic laundry bag I found in the bathroom. I hope your mother won't object to my borrowing it.'

'Of course not,' Sara said in the same down-to-earth, humourless voice without showing the wild laughter threatening to break out of her. He looked oddly helpless, hovering between anger and embarrassment. The sooner he could get away—from her, from the situation, from this disaster which had become of their apparently stable relationship—the sooner he could return to his usual placidity. Peter hated extremes of emotion, he was afraid of them, couldn't handle them.

'I hope your suit hasn't been ruined,' she said and then wished she could catch the words back. Peter didn't want to be reminded of those moments on the beach. He would want no reminders of her, either. Peter never talked about the girlfriends he had had; once they were gone, they vanished from his mind. He was a man who liked life comfortable and easy, the soil of his mind too shallow to allow anything to put down deep roots.

He looked at her and shrugged. 'Goodbye, Sara,' he said. 'I hope you know what you're doing.'

He was gone a second later and she watched him drive away, smiling at the sting in the final remark. He had had the last word. She felt that he had gone at once to make sure she didn't have a chance to retort. Peter's ego needed some sort of pick-me-up.

'Has he gone?' her mother asked as Sara came back into the house.

'Don't look so pleased, he's a nice man and he deserves better,' Sara said crossly.

'It was you who sent him away, not me,' her mother unanswerably told her. 'I won't pretend I'm not glad, I'm not a hypocrite. He wasn't the man for you.'

Sara went upstairs without answering; it was true, unfortunately, and she couldn't think of any come-back. She had come within a hair's breadth of making a monumental mistake. She and Peter had had nothing in common and she would never have looked at him if she hadn't been on the rebound from Alex.

Her parents were very quiet and tactful at dinner that evening, they didn't mention Peter or Alex or ask her any questions. Sara did the washing up and tidied the kitchen while her mother watched her favourite programme on the TV, and then Sara went to bed early, as much because she wanted to be alone as because she was tired. She put the light out at ten o'clock and lay in the warm darkness listening to the sleepy whisper of the wind among the trees, until she fell asleep.

She woke up to a delicious smell of coffee and opened her eyes lazily to find the room full of daylight and Alex.

She was wide awake in two seconds flat, almost knocking the cup of coffee out of his hand as she sprang up like a Jack-in-the-box.

'What are you doing in my bedroom?' He was casually dressed in an open neck shirt and grey pants and looked as if he had been awake for hours. The alert vibrancy of his personality made her head ache immediately. She felt too weak to take any more of Alex, especially when she had just woken up.

'Get out,' she said tersely, looking around for something to hit him with. He put her coffee down on the bedside table and sat on the bed as Sara tried to scramble out of it, planting his hands on the mattress on either side of her, trapping her between his arms.

He was too close. Sara shrank back against the pillow, yelling: 'Get out, I said! Mum! Mum!' How could her mother let him come up here? How could she do such a thing?

'She's out,' Alex said complacently. 'She had to go to the village to get some milk, she had run out.'

Sara didn't believe a word of it, but she saw that she was alone in this house with Alex, and that he had caught her in a very vulnerable position. She was only wearing the briefest pretence of a nightdress; white lawn, trimmed with lace, absurdly frivolous, dangerously low cut. Sara wished she was wearing something sensible that covered her from neck to toe. She wished Alex would stop staring at her with that look in his eyes. She wished her heart would stop beating so fast.

'If you insist on talking to me, go away and I'll get dressed,' she said nervously.

'And have you lock the door the minute I'm out of it?' he mocked. 'No way. I'm here and I'm staying and you're going to listen.'

'Oh, no, I'm not,' she said. 'I don't want to talk to you—I don't want to hear anything you have to say.'

He looked at her in silence and the pulse in her throat beat wildly as she tried to outstare him. His face was oddly pale and set, the black centres of his eyes burned harshly, with a feeling which made her body weak.

'Go away,' she whispered because she was suddenly afraid.

'I can't,' Alex said hoarsely. 'You know I can't let you go, Sara. It isn't possible, I couldn't bear it.'

She closed her eyes, swaying back against the pillows for a second, her skin cold with emotional shock and a pain which was too bitterly familiar.

'Don't touch me,' she cried as she felt him move beside the bed.

He halted, breathing raggedly. 'Listen to me, then—let me tell you what I came to tell you. You owe me that much. Surely you can at least listen?'

She swallowed, shivering. After a moment she

said: 'Well, what do you want to tell me?' It wouldn't make any difference, whatever he said, but she would listen and then he would walk out of her life forever.

CHAPTER TEN

ALEX sat down beside her and picked up the cup of coffee he had brought her. 'Sit up and drink this while it's still hot.'

Sara gingerly sat up, clutching the sheet to her, and accepted the cup. The coffee was strong and delicious, she sipped it while he watched, his lean body lounging casually close to her.

'I've never talked about my childhood, have I?' he said in a conversational tone and Sara gave him a startled look.

'You know you haven't.' He had never talked to her about so many things that she had wanted to know about. When you are in love you need to discover everything about the other; there is an intense desire to merge entirely, see with their eyes, become one being. It is part of the bonding that makes the pair, separates them from everyone else, cements their relationship. Alex had held back far too much of himself while Sara had hid nothing. There had been nothing to hide, of course; she had been too young, almost a clean sheet of paper on which Alex had written what he wished.

'I couldn't,' he said shortly. 'I still find it hard to talk about. I grew up in an orphanage, you know that.'

'Yes,' she said, watching him and totally intent now.

'My mother died when I was born, but I lied to you when I said she had no family—she had parents living then. Her father was a solicitor, very respectable and quite well off, but they refused to have me in the house when my mother died. You see, she wasn't married. They had no idea who the father was, she never told them. They were horrified when they found out that she was expecting a child, they sent her away to have it in the country, but she died the day after I was born. Her parents couldn't face the scandal of having an illegitimate grandchild so they placed me with an orphanage.'

Sara held her coffee cup, not daring to drink in case it disturbed him, hearing the hard note of anger and pain in his voice. He was pale and his face had set in lines of harsh tension.

'I hated that bloody place,' he said. 'The people who ran it weren't cruel but it was always cold and the food was disgusting, and you had to sleep in rooms full of other children. A lot of bullying went on, you had to be tough to hold your own. You didn't have anything that belonged to you; everything was shared. You wore clothes that had been someone else's first, you lived by a bell—it woke you up and kept you running all day until it told you to put out the light. If you made friends with other children they always seemed to be taken away—some were adopted, others went back to their real parents. I used to see children in the street when we went out for walks, ordinary children with parents. You could tell they were different. It's hard to explain—it's a look you see in their eyes. They aren't worried, I suppose that's the closest I can come to describing it.'

The coffee cup clattered in the saucer as Sara's hand shook and she jumped as if at some resounding crash. Alex absently took the cup and put it down, his eyes all black pupil. She watched that look, recognising it—was that the look he hadn't seen in the eyes of ordinary children?

'We lived in a grey little world of our own behind high walls—I've no doubt they thought it was a good place for kids, there was lots of room, a park with grass and trees around the house, a big toy room and swings in the garden. But there's something in the air of institutions that makes everything tasteless, lifeless. From the time I could think, I knew I wanted to get out of there. When I was twelve I broke into the orphanage office one night.' He caught the startled look in her eyes and gave her an ironic smile. 'No, I didn't steal anything—except information. They hadn't told me anything about myself except that my parents were dead and I had no family. I needed to know more than that but you know what kids are like—it didn't occur to me to ask anyone, I spent months wondering about it and at last I decided to find out for myself. I found my card and discovered I had grandparents living—I found their address, too. And that was when I found out I was illegitimate.'

'You didn't know until then?' she asked huskily.

He shrugged. 'The people who ran the orphanage believed in telling children as little as possible—I suppose I ought to be grateful to them for keeping that one bit of information from me, no doubt they meant well.'

'It must have been a shock,' she whispered, her hand moving towards him. He caught it and held it tightly.

'Oh, yes,' he said, his mouth crooked. 'But I had some crazy idea that if I found my grandparents they would welcome me with open arms. I suppose I thought they didn't realise where I was.'

Sara's eyes burned with hard unshed tears at the flat bitterness in his voice. She wound her fingers around his and felt his icy skin with an ache of pity.

'I ran away next day and found my grand-parents. They almost fainted. I can see their faces now; they didn't need to tell me that they didn't want me, I knew it. They sent for the police and I was taken back to the orphanage. The people there weren't unkind but I'd broken a rule and had to be punished—so they made me sweep up all the leaves on the lawns. It was October, it took me hours.' He gave her a wry look. 'I've never liked autumn much since then. After that, I had a few very bad years—I was taken to foster parents several times and ran away. I ran away from the orphanage, too. I was a difficult teenager and the last time I ran away they didn't bother to look for me very hard. I never went back, I got a job as a messenger boy in Wardour Street and that was the end of my childhood.'

'Why didn't you tell me all this years ago?' she asked and he gave her a twisted smile.

'I hated talking about it, still do.'

Tentatively she asked: 'Because you don't know who your father was?'

'Partly, but it isn't as simple as that—I was miserable as a child and I don't like remembering. Every time I see an autumn leaf I go cold—I hate the colours of autumn, the orange and gold and russet. I see leaves and I want to run away. You can't explain things like that easily, you can't alter them by knowing what it is that makes you react like that. They aren't reachable by reason, they just are, there at the bottom of your mind. I remember I once had to shoot a scene in a wood in autumn, it was a nightmare, I sweated over it, couldn't sleep for days until it was in the can, and then when the film came out all the critics said it was the best scene in the film. They raved about it and I couldn't admit that I always had to shut my eyes when I saw that scene on the screen. It made me sick.'

She remembered the scene. It was one that had made a big impression on her, too. The visual impact was oddly haunting, she had never quite been able to work out why, but now she guessed that Alex had layered the celluloid with his own emotions, using no words, only colour and form, like a painter. The scene had given depth to an otherwise superficial, commercial film.

'I never had a home until I met you,' he said, looking down at their entwined fingers. 'When I first got away from the orphanage I loved living alone, having my own bedroom, not having to share anything. For years I didn't want anything but that. Only someone who has lived cheek by jowl with dozens of other people for years can know what pleasure it is to be alone. I certainly didn't want to get married.' He gave her a suddenly reckless grin. 'I was having too good a time.'

'I see,' Sara said, her imagination far too inventive.

Alex read her eyes and smiled. 'Nobody meant a damn until I met you,' he assured her. 'Do you remember that day? You appeared at my door looking about fourteen, very shy and nervous, and I almost didn't ask you in because I knew on sight that I fancied you and I was afraid to ask how old you were. I was pretty sure I was twice your age, I thought I might be turning into a dirty old man.'

She laughed. 'Idiot.'

'You *were* too young, though,' he said, more soberly. 'Once you'd begun to relax you had a gaiety I envied. It's hard to explain, but there was a sort of bloom on you, a happy confidence, I suppose. You'd been loved and looked after all your life. You weren't spoilt, though—you were naturally sweet and generous, you lit up the house that day and I was afraid to let you find out too much about me. I felt like someone with an unmentionable disease; I'd never been happy in my life, I came from a grey, ugly world and you were from somewhere very different. I didn't want you to feel sorry for me. I wanted you to love me. I thought if I had you, I might find out at last how it felt . . . oh, it sounds crazy! I was looking for my childhood, Sara—as if I could experience everything I'd never had by being close to you.'

She drew a difficult breath. 'I do understand, it isn't crazy.'

He lifted her hand to his mouth and kissed it, his eyes closed. 'Yesterday, when you made fun of me, when I asked you to talk to me and you said I'd never talked to you, I saw my mistake. I hadn't wanted to let that grey world touch you, can you see that? But I'd just been holding too much of myself back, you hadn't realised how much you meant to me.'

'Tell me one other thing,' she said quietly, watching his brooding face. 'Why wouldn't you have children? Surely that would have made it a real home.'

He flushed darkly and his eyes opened, their dark centres dilated. 'I told myself it was because I didn't want anyone coming between us, but that wasn't the whole truth. Part of it, maybe, but not the whole truth. I wanted to be the centre of your world. If you'd had a child, that would have pushed me out. I'd have been outside again, watching an ordinary child in a happy family get what I didn't have, and I couldn't stand that.'

'Oh, Alex,' she said, and leaned her head against his chest, fighting with tears.

'Don't, darling,' he said huskily, his arms going round her.

'Why didn't you ever tell me before? When I left you, last year, why didn't you tell me then?'

He put his cheek against her hair, rocking her as though she were a child, and the irony of that hurt her. Throughout their marriage she had felt that Alex saw her as a child, and she had been right in one sense. She had raged against him for keeping her a child—how could she have guessed that Alex needed her the way she was, that she gave him something no other woman had ever given him? If she had realised, how would she have seen him then?

'I was too proud to admit how much I needed you,' he said, kissing her cloudy hair. 'I hated the idea of letting you see what you meant to me. I had to be strong, Sara, that was how you saw me, how I wanted you to see me. And anyway, I thought you'd come back. I didn't believe you would divorce me, at first, and I was angry with you for refusing to take my word that I hadn't had an affair with Madeleine. If you'd only known what a damn nuisance that woman was . . .'

He began to tell her the story she had already heard from LJ and she listened, her head against his shoulder, hearing the beating of his heart and the steady rise and fall of his chest just below her cheek.

'She had the idea I fancied her and when I made it clear I wasn't interested she turned nasty. Said I'd wrecked her marriage, let her believe that if she was free . . .' He shrugged distastefully. 'She made my hair curl. I talked to LJ and he took her off my hands. I thought that was the end of it but when I came home I found her husband had been down to see you and told you the story Madeleine had told him.'

'I wonder if she put the idea into his head,' Sara said thoughtfully.

'I wouldn't put it past her. LJ tells me she's got her hooks into a politician now; his marriage is heading for the rocks and Madeleine is waiting for the crash. She's an ambitious lady.'

'When you asked me to take your word, you were testing me, weren't you?' she said quietly. He had demanded proof that she would go on loving him whatever happened, whatever he did; that unchanging, unquestioning love a mother gives a child. 'You didn't want to explain because you wanted to be shown I trusted you.'

He hadn't been thinking rationally, but then love wasn't rational. He had been feeling with an intensity that betrayed the depth of his need for love—and that made her ache with regret for having failed him, for ever having left him. Yet hadn't it been inevitable? Alex hadn't wanted her to grow up, he had tried to keep her exactly as she had been when he first met her, yet he had wanted an adult love from her and that was an irreconcilable contradiction.

By leaving him and rapidly growing up over a year of loneliness, pain and self-discovery, she had resolved the situation herself, away from him. If he had told her all of this five years ago she would have been puzzled, worried and probably reluctant to get involved with him. Maybe his instincts had been right, after all. He couldn't tell her or he would lose her—so he had constructed a dream world for them both and it had worked for four years.

'Then you left me and started divorce proceedings and I still thought it would be okay as soon as I saw you again,' he said. 'I tried to make you see me but you were surprisingly obstinate, I couldn't provoke you into meeting me again.' He looked at her through lowered lashes, frowning. 'And then you met another guy and your family told me they were afraid you would marry him. That was the biggest shock, that was when I began to think about you in a different way, and think about myself and realise what a crazy way I'd been behaving. I was still struggling through, towards going to you, telling you how much I loved you, when you had that accident and they rang and told me. It wasn't until I walked into the room and you ran into my arms that it dawned on me that something had happened to your memory, that you didn't remember the divorce.'

'And, quick as a flash, you decided to take advantage of the situation,' she said drily and he watched her with rueful eyes.

'It was unscrupulous, I know, but it looked like my last chance! I had to know if you still loved me—you were in shock when I drove you back from the hospital, I didn't think I could be sure of anything from the way you acted then. I thought if we could go back for a little while, have a breathing space and get to know each other again, I might find out how you really felt. I could see that you had changed—you weren't the girl I'd married, being away from you for a year showed me how big a difference there was, but I couldn't believe you really cared about the other guy.'

'No,' she said in a low voice, frowning.

He watched her intently. 'You didn't, did you?' There was the faintest thread of uncertainty in his voice and she registered it and gave him a wry smile.

'No, Alex. I tried to care for him, I even convinced myself I did for a while, but I'm afraid it was just a mistake.' She pushed a lock of black hair back from his cheek, her hand gentle. 'My mother told you he had gone, didn't she? You knew before you came up here.'

He gave her a quick look. 'Yes, she rang me last night and told me.'

'And the two of you plotted a lightning strike before I got away again?' she said with accusing impatience. 'Wait until I see her again!'

'Don't be angry with her, she loves you. She said to me last night that it was time I talked to you honestly. You'd said something to her about not being treated as an adult, she thought I might have shut you out and kept my own counsel and she thought that that was what was wrong between us, not so much Madeleine, as the way I treated you.'

'She was right,' Sara said, surprised. 'I hardly knew a thing about you, did I?'

'It will never be that way again,' he promised quickly.

'Did my parents know about your background?' she asked, jealous of the idea that he might have talked to them when he wouldn't talk to her, but he shook his head.

'Not even LJ knows the whole story, although I've told him some of it. He's always been like a father to me, you know that, I confided in him years ago.'

She smiled at him. 'He's a marvellous man— did you know that he came to see me the other day?'

Alex stared at her, taken aback. 'Did he? When? What did he say?' He listened, frowning, as she told him. 'Damn him, he had no business to interfere,' he said. 'He could have done more harm than good. I wanted to tell you the truth about Madeleine myself.' His frown deepened. 'Is that why you said that you believed me now? Yesterday? When you said it didn't matter anyway?'

She nodded. 'It didn't matter whether it was true or not because I'd realised that Madeleine wasn't the real problem—it was you.'

He looked at her anxiously. 'And now?' Before she could open her mouth to reply he said hurriedly, with a husky agitation: 'I love you, Sara, come back to me. We'll live where you like. If you want to live in London . . .'

'None of that matters, when you wouldn't take me to London with you it didn't upset me because I loved London but because I felt you were always shutting me out of the most important part of your life.'

'Darling, *you* were the most important thing in my life,' he said, a flare of red along his cheekbones and his eyes darkening with passion.

'Was I?' She searched his eyes for the truth and he groaned, staring back at her, his face vulnerable with love.

'Don't you know that? None of the rest of it matters. You make the world a place I can live in—until I met you, I lived inside my work, but although I still love making films, they haven't been first with me since you came into my life.' He bent his head and pressed his heated mouth into her bare shoulder, running kisses along the delicate bones, pushing his face into the hollow of her throat.

She trembled, closing her desire-drowsy eyes, wanting him more than she ever had before. Their lovemaking in the past had been limited by her inexperience and youth, and Alex's care not to disturb either. They hadn't touched the heights or plumbed the depths of love; he had been afraid to take her to either in case it shattered that dream they shared. Now she was a woman with no trace of the child left in her. She pulled Alex down on to the bed, moving urgently, her fingers hurried as she unbuttoned his shirt.

'I love you,' she muttered, searching for his lips, and under her hands she felt the sudden crash of his quickening heartbeat.

He kissed her with a hunger that became sensual, his mouth slow and hot, caressing her parted lips with a passion he was trying to control. Alex was still holding back, half afraid to loose the emotion locked inside him.

'Love me,' she whispered, her hands running over his cool, smooth skin, arching against him invitingly, and felt laughter shake him.

'I'm going to,' he promised.

She slid down his body, her teeth grazing lightly where they touched, and felt the gasp of shaken surprise as her mouth incited and teased. He had to recognise now that she was a woman, not a child, he had to give and take in uninhibited sensual passion; there must be no shelter for either of them any more. Only when they knew

each other in the wordless intimacy where there
are no pretences or disguises, no need to explain
or question, no doubts or uncertainties, would
their love have a safe future.

'Darling, you're driving me crazy,' Alex said
feverishly, moving against her in increasing
urgency. 'I love you.' He arched over her, staring
down at her flushed and inviting face as if he had
never seen it before, and she ran her hands down
his tense body in a silken movement that made
his eyes burn.

'I love you,' she whispered and then he came
down to her with a gasped desire that drove
everything from her head but the pleasure he was
giving her. They had never made love with such
intensity before and she discovered a new
sensitivity in her flesh, a piercing excitement that
wrung moans of almost agonised sensuality from
her. They made love as if on the edge of an abyss,
as if for the last time; the nervous tension of their
long separation stretching out the moments of
mounting fever until the wire that held them both
snapped and they fell over the edge, shuddering
with release.

They lay on the bed, hot and trembling, so
exhausted that they were almost asleep when they
heard the discreetly noisy slam of the front door
and Mrs Calthrop's footsteps as she walked
through the hall to the kitchen. Sara stirred, her
limbs heavy and moist with perspiration.

'My mother,' she whispered, yawning.

Alex stretched, his body sliding against her
naked flesh and making her senses quiver.

'We'd better get up and dress,' she said.

'Hmm.' His hand wandered down the satin curve of her hip. 'Must we?'

'Yes, we must,' she said, smiling, but slapping his hand away.

He groaned and sat up, his lean body powerful as he swung off the bed and began to collect his clothes and dress while she lay and watched, her eyes lazy.

'We ought to have a second honeymoon,' Alex thought aloud, viewing her drily as he buttoned his shirt under her inspection. 'Stop looking at me like that unless you want me to take these clothes off and join you.'

She put her hands under her head, one knee raised in casual relaxation. 'Any minute now my mother may come up. Honeymoon where?'

'I know an isolated little cottage where we wouldn't have any visitors and could stay in bed all day if we liked,' he suggested.

'Would we like?' Sara considered, her head to one side and her gaze wandering over him.

'I'd make sure we did,' Alex promised. 'We need a few days alone to talk and decide what we're going to do.'

'About what?'

'All sorts of things—where to live, whether you want to stay on at your job, when we start a family.' Alex saw the change in her face, the laziness gone and a sombre look in her eyes.

'Not yet, Alex,' she said gently. 'You know I want one badly, I'd love a baby, but I don't think you're ready for that yet and I want to make sure we both want our baby when it arrives. As to my job, I'd like to go on working there—when you're abroad on location work I'd have something to keep me busy and stop me missing you too much. We've got a lot of work to do on our marriage— don't let's rush anything. This time we have a fighting chance of making it a real marriage, not a daydream. The real family can come later. First, let's find each other.'

She had to face the possibility that he might never want a child, but that was something they had to find out together, she couldn't blackmail him into giving in on anything so important. It wouldn't be fair to any of them, herself or Alex, or their child.

He knelt on the bed and took her face between his hands. 'I love you, Sara,' he said huskily and she smiled with wavering tenderness at him.

'Nothing else matters,' she promised.

Coming Next Month in Harlequin Presents!

855   A FOREVER AFFAIR   Rosemary Carter
Despite its savage beauty, her husband's African game reserve is
no longer home. Was it carved in stone that she could never love
another man? Surely a divorce would change that!

856   PROMISE OF THE UNICORN   Sara Craven
To collect on a promise, a young woman returns her talisman—
the protector of virgins—to its original owner. The power of the
little glass unicorn was now with him!

857   AN IRRESISTIBLE FORCE   Ann Charlton
A young woman is in danger of being taken over by a subtle
irresistible force rather than by open aggression when she takes
on an Australian construction king who's trying to buy out her
grandmother.

858   INNOCENT PAWN   Catherine George
Instead of looking past the money to the man behind it, a mother
is prompted by panic to blame her husband when their five-year-
old daughter is kidnapped.

859   MALIBU MUSIC   Rosemary Hammond
California sunshine and her sister's beach house provide the
atmosphere a young woman needs to focus on her future—until
her neighbor tries to seduce her.

860   LADY SURRENDER   Carole Mortimer
The man who bursts into her apartment can't see why his best
friend would throw away his marriage for a woman like her. But
soon he can't imagine any man—married or otherwise—*not*
falling for her.

861   A MODEL OF DECEPTION   Margaret Pargeter
A model takes on an assignment she can't handle when she tries
to entice a man into selling his island in the Caribbean. She was
supposed to deceive the man, not fall in love.

862   THE HAWK OF VENICE   Sally Wentworth
Most people travel to Venice to fall in love. Instead, an au pair girl
makes the journey to accuse a respected Venetian count of
kidnapping—or of seduction, at least.

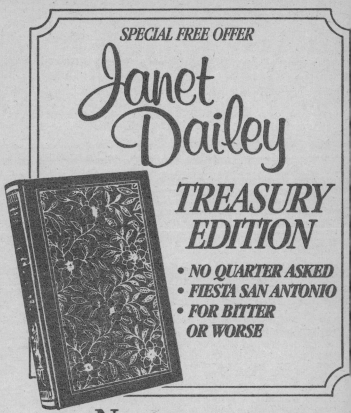

Here's how to get this special offer from Harlequin!
As simple as 1...2...3!

BONUS
TREASURY EDITION
COUPON

1. Each month, save one Treasury Edition coupon from your favorite Romance or Presents novel.
2. In four months you'll have saved four Treasury Edition coupons (<u>only one coupon per month allowed</u>).
3. Then all you have to do is fill out and return the order form provided, along with the four Treasury Edition coupons required and $1.00 for postage and handling.

Mail to: Harlequin Reader Service

In the U.S.A.
2504 West Southern Ave.
Tempe, AZ 85282

In Canada
P.O. Box 2800, Postal Station A
5170 Yonge Street
Willowdale, Ont. M2N 6J3

Please send me my FREE copy of the Janet Dailey Treasury Edition. I have enclosed the four Treasury Edition coupons required and $1.00 for postage and handling along with this order form.

(Please Print)

NAME_____

ADDRESS_____

CITY_____

STATE/PROV._____ZIP/POSTAL CODE_____

SIGNATURE_____
This offer is limited to one order per household.

This special Janet Dailey offer expires January 1986.

SUPPLIES LIMITED

Eye of the Storm

Maura Seger

A powerful portrayal of the events of World War II in the Pacific, *Eye of the Storm* is a riveting story of how love triumphs over hatred. In this, the first of a three-book chronicle, Army nurse Maggie Lawrence meets Marine Sgt. Anthony Gargano. Despite military regulations against fraternization, they resolve to face together whatever lies ahead.... Author Maura Seger, also known to her fans as Laurel Winslow, Sara Jennings, Anne MacNeil and Jenny Bates, was named 1984's Most Versatile Romance Author by *The Romantic Times*.

Take 4 novels and a surprise gift FREE